Now.

It had to be now. Kill them and then get away clean.

They were waiting for him. The way the gooks had waited for him in the village in Nam.

They were only women. Like that little gook in Nam. And she hadn't given him too hard a time.

He could take care of both of them.

Now.

At the door to the hall, he stopped and ran over in his mind the layout of the house. Every room had two doors. He could come in one, and they'd go out the other.

He smiled. It would make it harder, and maybe that would be more fun. The house was like a maze. It had the mice, and it had the cat now. Cat and mouse.

And he was the cat.

The mice were just waiting. Waiting for the cops to come and release them from the trap.

He felt something strange at the edge of his mind. As if a cold finger had been laid against his temple. He frowned and shook his head and felt the sweat trickle down his side. He felt chilled. His heart was pounding again.

Slowly, he made his way toward the hallway. But just as he was almost into the hall, the finger against his temple became an icy hand that felt as if it were scrabbling at the back of his neck. He stifled a scream and crouched in the alcove, shaking, his eyes straining with fear, sweat dripping into them.

It was in this fog of fear that he heard, as if from a long distance, the back door close, the bolt-lock click into place, and the key grate as it was removed from the lock.

The Crystal Curtain

by
Sandy Bayer

Boston • Alyson Publications, Inc.

Published as a trade paperback original
by Alyson Publications
40 Plympton Street
Boston, Mass. 02118.

Distributed in the U.K. by GMP Publishers,
PO Box 247, London, N15 6RW, England.

First U.S. edition: June, 1988

ISBN 1-55583-123-0
LC 87-072877

Dedicated to
Cecilia Ford Prince,
who convinced me that the dream
could be a reality,

and
Rebecca Jean Lee,
who helps me keep it a reality

The Crystal Curtain

Prolog

1945

Carol Brubaker set the mug of steaming coffee on one of the small round tables in the nurses' lounge and settled her plump body into a straight-backed chair. Propping her feet on the chair next to her, she released a tired sigh. She was tucking a few blond wisps of hair back under her cap when the door opened behind her. She turned slightly.

"It's still snowing, Henny." Carol glanced toward the windows on the far side of the room.

In the blackness outside, heavy swirls of snow swept across the glass. The wind blasted a flurry against the windows and then retreated, leaving them rattling in their frames. Carol shivered and rubbed her bare arms.

"Yeah, it's a real lulu, all right." Henrietta Pryor popped a couple of coins into the Coke machine and immediately smacked the heel of her hand against the coin slot, as if from long habit. The machine whirred, clicked, and thudded a bottle into the trough. "Boston might be dug out sometime in August."

"How can you drink that and still stay so thin?"

"Metabolism." She sat down at the table.

Carol grimaced. "I should have such overactive glands."

"Stop worrying about your weight. You're as healthy as a horse."

"Thanks. That's just what I needed to hear."

"Oh, hell, you know what I mean. Look, what's on your mind? You're so jumpy tonight."

Carol fiddled with her cup for a minute, frowning. Then she glanced at the dark-haired woman sitting across from her.

"The Nowland baby."

"What about her?" Henrietta sipped at the Coke.

"Haven't you noticed how sensitive she is to everything?"

"You're the one who's been hovering over her like a mother hen."

Carol shrugged. "I know, but there's something funny. Billingsley walked in just after we came on shift, and that poor baby almost rolled up in a ball — like she was protecting herself. And it's not the first time it's happened."

"Well, she's not the only one who tenses up when our precious head nurse makes a royal appearance. I get pretty tight myself." Henrietta stood and headed for the cookie-and-cracker machine. "Besides, babies are sensitive to the way people touch them. Billingsley has all the warmth of a cobra."

"No." Carol frowned. "If that were it, I probably wouldn't have even noticed. Billingsley doesn't have to touch her. She just has to walk into the nursery."

Henrietta came back to the table and unwrapped a package of cheese-and-peanut-butter crackers. "You're making a mountain out of a molehill, Carol. I went in last night, and she started bawling like I was going to hit her. Two hours later, she gurgled at me like I was Santa Claus and it was Christmas Eve. Maybe she's just a little colicky."

Carol chuckled. "Hogwash. When you came in last night, you'd just had a fight with Joe. You were ready to chew nails."

Henrietta opened her mouth, but Carol shushed her. "He called two hours later and you made up. Then you went back to the nursery with this absolutely *dreamy* look on your face."

Henrietta dismissed the observation with a wave of her hand, but her face had pinkened.

"I tell you," Carol said with more intensity, "that baby *knew*. She felt you were different."

Henrietta took another bite of the cracker, chewed for a minute, and washed it down with Coke. Finally, she sighed in resignation.

"Okay. I know when you set your mind to something, nothing's going to change it. So maybe you're right. Maybe she's more sensitive." She brushed a few crumbs from the table into her hand and dusted them into the ashtray. "*Maybe.*"

Silent, Carol stared into her coffee. With the tip of her finger, she traced the dark-stained crack from the lip of the white ceramic mug halfway down its side.

Henrietta leaned back and studied her. "So what else is it?"

"Nothing." Carol gave an unconvincing shrug.

"I know you better than that. You've got something eating at you."

Carol sighed. "It's crazy."

"You mean crazier than the Nowland kid?"

"Well, it's something else that happened with her." She fiddled with the cup for several more seconds. "What it is — " She took a deep breath and let it out before she met the other woman's penetrating gaze. "I was changing the Ryan boy's diapers a little while ago. My back was to her, and all of a sudden, I got this funny feeling that somebody was — well, like somebody was watching me."

Henrietta snorted. "You mean somebody like the Nowland baby?"

Carol nodded and looked toward the windows in order to avoid Henrietta's eyes. Ice was forming in the corners of the panes. She shivered again.

"You're right," Henrietta said. "That's crazy. She can't even focus her eyes yet."

"I know that. I told you it was crazy. And it wasn't her eyes." She met Henrietta's piercing stare again. "I felt her touching me."

"*Touching* you? Come on, Carol — "

"I know. But I felt — it was like her — her mind was reaching out and sort of *patting* me. You know, the way an older baby pats your face or hair when you're holding it. It felt like she was — inside my head." She shook her head. "It's hard to explain."

For long minutes then, Carol stared into the cup as if she were reading tea leaves. Henrietta watched her from the table. The silence was broken only by the whoosh and rattle of the icy wind against the windows.

Finally, Henrietta pushed back her chair, stood, and picked up the wrapper and Coke bottle. She plunked the bottle into the wooden case of empties behind the door and tossed the wrapper into the trash can.

"Well, I think you ought to just forget about it, Carol." She opened the door. "I think the graveyard shift is getting to you. It's a little spooky up here sometimes."

Carol nodded silently, but she did not turn to face Henrietta.

The door closed.

She took a sip of coffee and frowned at the snow that billowed across the windows.

No matter what Henrietta said, it was true.

The baby had touched her.

She had felt it.

Part One

The dashboard lights of the old Ford cast a greenish glow on Frank Talbot's face as he sped along the deserted county blacktop. His sinewy hands, white-knuckled, gripped the steering wheel.

Talbot shot a glance at Danny Alcott, slumped against the passenger door, his head lolling with the bends in the road.

A smile crept across Talbot's thin, hard mouth. Danny would be out for hours. The big, stupid kid had never been able to hold his liquor.

It was a weakness that was going to save Frank Talbot from Georgia's little white room of death.

In the back seat, Betty Jean Warren's body sprawled where Talbot had killed her. Flowers of dark blood blossomed across her partially nude body. Her glassy eyes stared upward, and her pink mouth was open as if in faint surprise. Her skirt was twisted obscenely around her slender waist.

Talbot stared into the blackness ahead, straining to see past the headlights. He fumbled on the seat for the bottle, lifted it to his lips, and spilled whiskey down his chin and onto his blood-streaked shirt. He dragged his arm across his mouth and cursed under his breath.

The Banner Creek cutoff was close. He slowed, looking for the break in the scrub pines that lined the road. As he spotted it, headlights of an oncoming car crested the hill just beyond the cutoff, and he jabbed at the accelerator again. When the tiny red lights winked out in the rearview mirror, he wrenched the car onto the gravel shoulder, swung over into the opposite lane, and started back. Cold sweat dripped down his sides and dampened his shirt. He licked at dry lips.

If no one saw him, he would have a chance.

The car squeaked and groaned as he turned onto the dirt-and-gravel road. Now, old pines groped their way out of the thick underbrush and towered on both sides.

A mile into the cutoff, Talbot stopped the car and turned off the lights. The blackness and silence engulfed him, made him feel safer.

He reached for the bottle again, his lean, muscular body relaxing slightly. The fear began to subside. But with the dwindling of the fear, the rage shot through him once more, and his hands clenched into rock-hard fists.

Damn silly bitch. Stinking whore.

She had asked for it, he told himself. There in the car with Danny passed out in the front seat. A *real* man was going to give her what she wanted. Not some snotty-nosed kid, but a *man*. She'd have begged for it if she had known how good it would've been. Would've gotten down on her knees and *begged* him to fuck her. His jaw muscle twitched spastically. But no, she had to get uppity. He pursed his mouth into a mimicking whine. *No, Frank, please, Frank, you're hurting me, Frank.* He turned the bottle up again and then wiped his mouth.

They were all whores.

Some of them tried to cover it up, but underneath they were all the same. His old man had told him that, and it was true. Even the one who was supposed to have been his mother. The one who'd run away when he was only two years old. Even she had been one. His jaw muscle worked again.

Betty Jean's dimestore perfume wafted up, mingling with the sharp, coppery smell of her blood. He rolled down the window, leaned his head out and gulped the cold, fresh air, forcing the sourness back down his throat. When his stomach had quieted, he lifted the bottle again and then stopped. It would be stupid to get drunk. He poured the rest of the whiskey out the window and heaved the bottle across the road.

Only afterwards did he realize his mistake. He smacked his fist against the steering wheel in irritation. What if they searched out here and found it? His fingerprints would be all over it. Of course, he considered, they wouldn't know when he'd thrown it there — maybe some time when he was heading up to the creek to do some fishing, he could say. Still, there was no point in having to explain anything he didn't have to.

He swung the car door open and stumbled across the road. Loose gravel rolled under his boots as he slid down the slight embankment into the ditch. Digging blindly through the tangle of dead limbs and undergrowth, he cursed bitterly, his hands and face clawed by brambles.

Then, as the futility of his efforts became apparent, the fear slithered back, a sick feeling in the pit of his stomach. He was beginning to feel that he was being watched. He jerked his head toward a sound in the brush a few feet away and tried to push down his panic at the feeling that there were eyes all around him, staring at him, watching him.

He began backing out of the undergrowth, the fear crawling up his spine now, his breath becoming more rapid. He could always come back later and get the goddamned bottle. Another sudden sound in the brush, a rustle of leaves, and he whirled and began clawing his way up the bank, terror pounding at his chest.

But once he reached the road, it took him only seconds to convince himself that no fear had propelled him there. It was just that there were more important things to take of right now. His breathing slowed, and he rubbed his jaw gingerly where a thorn had gouged him. He stared toward the car.

It was just that there were more important things to take care of. Fear had nothing to do with it.

1984
Thursday
26
April

1

Stephanie Nowland stood beside what was left of the ravaged body lying face down in the damp pine needles and reluctantly allowed the flood of psychic impressions to swell and engulf her.

She forced herself to know the knife almost as intimately as Betty Jean Warren had known it. The slashing into the soft flesh of her abdomen, the grating of steel against bone as it glanced off her lower rib, tearing into muscle, finally ripping into her heart with an ugly twist. Driving in hard, over and over and over. A painful sob rose in Stephanie's throat, but she pushed it back.

Later, small scurrying animals had torn at Betty Jean's flesh in their own way.

Stephanie turned away, barely controlling the violent lurching of her stomach. She sucked deeply at the dark, earth-smelling air and shivered in her raincoat. Shoving her fists into the pockets, she wished that she had zipped in the lining before leaving the motel and wondered if she would be warm again before she got back to Saint Augustine.

To her left, through heavy underbrush and up the embankment, blue lights revolved eerily on the tops of three patrol cars that had been pulled off the road and pointed into the black woods. Their headlights glared through the trees, as if keeping their prey in sight. Ten or twelve other cars and pickup trucks lined the road.

Shadowy figures huddled in groups, perhaps twenty men and fewer than half a dozen women. When they passed in front of the headlights, they looked ghostly; floating apparitions in the terrible night. She knew they were tired now, those who had searched for the young woman, and they wanted to go home to late, warmed-over suppers and hot showers.

And yet, some fascination with death and evil kept them here.

Around her, in every other direction, dark, rain-streaked pines marched into the desolate blackness, away from the horror they had witnessed.

Stephanie trudged back toward the road, shielding her eyes from the lights. Her jeans were heavy, damp to the knees from the wet underbrush that tore at her legs, and she felt uncomfortable and incredibly tired.

Two men passed her, one carrying a black body bag. Their faces were hidden in shadows, but her mind was going out now — probing, seeking — and she touched the grimness and revulsion they felt for their task.

The man who carried the bag turned toward her, startled, his face and the fear on it suddenly etched sharply in the harsh light. She averted her eyes and walked on, regretting his fear, surprised that he had sensed the touch. Few were aware of it when it was accidental, as it had been this time.

The other man called to his friend, *Jimmy?*, puzzled at his halt in their journey and the stiffness of his body.

Dr. Michael Turner met her halfway up the embankment with an extended hand and pulled her up to the road. Part-time coroner for the south Georgia county, he reminded her of the ruggedly handsome men in the Marlboro advertisements. But his eyes were too sensitive, she thought. The autopsy would be difficult.

"Can I give you a lift back to the motel? You look exhausted." He turned up the collar of his light jacket. The sunny April afternoon had been deceptively warm.

Stephanie shook her head. "Thanks, Mike. I'll be okay."

Turner glanced toward the woods. "Yeah, I guess we'll all be okay."

They were convenient lies, clung to for reassurance in a lonely, soulless place.

Sheriff Ray Dempsey loomed out of the darkness, his big shoulders hunched against the chilling dampness. In contrast to those of the young coroner, Dempsey's eyes, overhung with graying eyebrows, looked as if they had seen far too much.

She knew the ridicule he had faced because Betty Jean's parents had called her for help when he had not been able to find their daughter, and she felt respect for him. What might have been felt as a severe blow to his pride and authority was accepted by Dempsey with a quiet dignity.

He touched her shoulder awkwardly. "Stephanie, I just want to thank you for all your help. It would've been a damn sight harder without you."

"Let me know if there is anything I can do, Sheriff."

Dempsey cleared his throat, as if embarrassed. "Well, I know you're tired now, and I don't want to keep imposing on you—"

"Whatever I can do."

"Well, if you think of anything that could point a finger at the man who did this, I'd surely appreciate it if you'd call me."

Stephanie looked toward the woods and watched the two men struggling with their grisly burden. Sleep would be difficult for her tonight. Faces would haunt her, would be joined by yet another one.

"Look for a dark blue jacket," she said, as the mental images became more sharply defined. Her hands almost felt the material sliding under her fingers — slippery, cool. "Probably a light nylon windbreaker."

Her eyes held Dempsey's briefly before she turned away again. "The knife will be in the right-hand pocket."

2

While the search party broke up on the Banner Creek cutoff, Frank Talbot slouched on his rumpled bed in the boarding house in the middle of Johnson and nursed a bottle of cheap bourbon. Scattered across the bed were *Soldier of Fortune* magazines opened to ads for survivalist clothing, food, weapons of death.

His steel-gray eyes stared vacantly at the small black-and-white television on the scarred dresser. But he wasn't seeing the images that flicked across the screen or hearing the hysterical squeals as another contestant won the brand-new 1984 Chevy Chevette.

On the screen of his mind, little yellow men crumpled as he shoved the bayonet into their stomachs, pushed them backwards, and jerked the bayonet out again. Their blood made tiny rivulets in the dust.

He and the other men in his company — those who were left after the minefields had blown most of them into bloody pieces — had crouched in the tall grass just outside the Vietnamese village until they were sure they had surprise on their side. Week-old sweat made them itch, their legs were cramped from hunkering down in the grass, and buzzing insects attacked their faces, necks and hands.

Then they were up and storming toward the little thatched huts, scattering themselves and their shouts across the clearing.

The young men, perhaps the only enemy, had fled to the jungle, leaving the old people, the women and the children. But it didn't matter any more who the real enemy was. What mattered was killing "little yellow gooks."

He found her in one of the dirt-floor huts, clutching a yowling baby against her breasts. When she saw him in the doorway, she whimpered. He imagined he smelled her fear of him, and he laughed, a soft growl in his throat.

He gestured with the bayonet for her to put the baby down. She shook her head back and forth, her long black hair waving across her face. He walked over to her and grinned. With one short, swift movement, he pierced the baby through, from side to side. With another abrupt movement, he dropped it from the bloody weapon into the dust.

It was quiet in the hut. The only sounds were the horrified mother crawling toward her dead infant and the twenty-year-old soldier's heavy breathing. He heard the pop of rifles on the other side of the village, but it was a dreamlike sound, unreal, far away.

He motioned with the tip of the blood-sheathed bayonet for her to stop. When she reached to gather up her child, he swung the rifle butt up and cracked it cruelly against her slim shoulder. She sprawled backwards, screaming in pain and terror. He detached the bayonet and held it at her throat while he tore at her clothes to search for weapons. There were none.

But when he pulled back, she wasn't just a little yellow gook to be killed. She was a woman with a ripe young body. His breathing grew rapid, shallow. When she saw his eyes, she began backing away from him on her hands and knees, watching him.

He wiped his hand across his mouth and stared at her, at the rise and fall of her bared breasts as she tried to get to her feet. He felt himself growing hard, felt his pulse race. He laughed softly, moved forward to corner her, and ripped at the pajama-like trousers.

Throwing her to the ground, he fell on her and pinned her beneath him. He held her slender wrists in a powerful, one-handed grip while he fumbled at the buttons on his fly. She struggled, jerking her body back and forth under him, understanding too late that it was only exciting him more.

He entered her, brutally, and smiled at the surprised pain that flickered in her eyes. He started pumping at her, riding between her tight, slim thighs.

Then, suddenly, she lay still. She looked up at him, her eyes hard, resigned, perspiration dotting her forehead from the pain and her struggle.

But she didn't move.

Move, damn you, you whore, move!

He slapped her face. But still she did not move. She lay under him and stoically took the stunning blows that increased in force with his frustration and rage.

Until his hand closed on the bayonet in the dirt beside him and he plunged it into her abdomen.

Then she moved.

She convulsed with pain, her eyes wide with terror. He felt his organ pulsing with power. So he stabbed her again. And as her body jerked one final, agonized time, he shot his semen into her. He heard a soft scream in the distance and only vaguely realized that the scream had his voice.

A shadow fell across the floor of the hut. He flung himself away from her body and faced the door, crouching, animal-like. The bayonet dripped still-warm blood onto his hand.

The lieutenant.

The young officer's mouth twisted with revulsion, mirroring his disgust. And then he spun stiffly on his heel and bolted from the hut.

In the days that followed, the lieutenant said nothing about the incident, but every time their eyes met, Talbot saw the judgment.

Soon he began to feel those eyes on him everywhere. They became a prison, the stuff of his nightmares. He would awake in the terrifying blackness with sweat chilling his body, shivering, his teeth chattering, his eyes wide with his fear.

But within a month, he was shipped home, and in Johnson, Georgia, he didn't have to see those eyes. In fact, by the time he arrived in Johnson, he had begun to see that the lieutenant was weak. A rich-assed bastard who probably still wanted to suck his momma's tits.

Weak.

Coming home was not what Talbot had expected it to be. There was no fanfare when he stepped off the bus from Atlanta, no one to meet him, slap him on the back, and welcome him home. Like the rest of the country, Johnson was trying to forget. Even those who had gone through the war were trying to forget, it seemed.

Frank Talbot wanted to remember.

In war, he had proved to himself that he was a man.

A few months after he had settled in, he and two of his friends had spent the day fishing at the creek. As the sun dipped below the trees and cast long shadows across the dark, gurgling water, they passed a bottle around until they were comradely drunk.

He told them about the woman in the hut. He felt the rush of power again as he relived the memory, knowing these men would understand what it had been like for him. After all, they had been there, too, and they were like him. They had grown up together, gone hunting together. They had even pooled their money one night before they were shipped out and bought a whore for an hour. They were like him.

But after a while, in the fading light, he saw their eyes grow sick, and one of them finally stood up abruptly and said, "It's time to go home."

After they left, he sat by himself in the dark for hours. If his old man had been alive, he would have understood.

He had smiled then in the black night. There was nothing they could do to him. And he knew they wouldn't talk. They were as weak as the lieutenant.

But now, lying on the bed in his boarding house room, Talbot raged inside.

That bitch was here.

In the ghostly, flickering light of the television set, he saw the shadow fall across the floor of the hut, saw the sick look in the eyes of the lieutenant, in the eyes of his friends.

Somehow, she was supposed to be able to see everything. And there would be no reason for her to keep quiet.

A folding hunting knife gleamed dully in his hand. He rubbed his thumb along the polished, inlaid-wood handle.

And then he stabbed the knife into the bed and pulled it out, over and over and over.

3

Back in the motel, Stephanie pulled the drapes across the sliding glass doors that opened onto the small terrace and the leaf-strewn pool beyond. She unwrapped a glass, fished melting ice from the Styrofoam bucket, and filled the glass with water from a plastic pitcher. As she lifted the glass to her lips, she met her own eyes in the mirror over the veneer-topped dresser. The sight jolted her.

She stared at the circles under the dark-brown eyes, darker than usual in the dim light of the dresser lamp, sunken too far into the softly angular face. She combed her fingers through her hair; stray silver glinted among the short, dark waves. The jagged scar across her jaw was livid. She looked haggard, considerably older than her thirty-nine years.

She lifted the glass again, the eyes in the mirror still holding hers.

How many nights had she spent alone in rooms like this one — feeling cold inside, fighting the loneliness? How many bodies had she found? How many killers?

She wanted to be with the living.

She wanted to sit with Mrs. Berkley, whose husband had died a year ago, and to reassure the elderly woman that her life was still worth living, that she wouldn't end up alone in the dreaded "old folk's home." She wanted to see Ron Pilcher, who always came worrying over his latest romance. She wanted to help Betty Farley find the courage to overcome the deranged cells loose in her body, to let the still-young woman know that she had a chance to see her small daughter grow to adulthood.

But her power called her too often to the dead.

When they couldn't find the killer — or sometimes the victim.

She moved to the bed, sank down on the edge, and sipped the water.

She knew that she could refuse. She could stay home and wake up every morning next to Marian's warm body and sleepy smile instead of the strangeness of another lonely room in Denver or Newark — or Johnson, Georgia.

But, occasionally, the phone would ring, and she would sit and stare at it for a long time — would dread answering it — knowing the caller was a man whose wife had dropped out of sight one morning while she was shopping. Or, like this time, it would be the parents of someone like Betty Jean Warren.

And she would finally pick up the receiver, and as the voice on the other end talked, she would feel her stomach drop, her shoulders tighten again.

Then she would find herself in another room like this one.

She stared at the carpet, and after several minutes she became aware of a stain just in front of her. She found herself intent upon its color and shape — dark, reddish brown, oval. She sipped more water, still watching the stain. She began to wonder what had been spilled, who had spilled it, why it could not be cleaned. She felt a sudden urge to get down on her hands and knees and scrub this spot. It was a nice carpet, really, she thought. Not beautiful, certainly, but pleasant. Nice blue-and-brown pattern.

And here was this terrible stain spoiling it.

Suddenly, she felt chilled. Her hands were shaking, the water was spilling over the rim of the glass onto the back of her hand. She set the glass down hard on the night table beside the bed and lay down.

She curled up, her knees pulling toward her chest, her eyes closed tightly, and from a place way down inside of her, she felt the sound start.

A sound of terror, of panic.

It crept from her abdomen into her stomach, filled her chest, and when it reached her throat, she opened her mouth and allowed it to come into the cold room.

It was a quiet sound, really — a cry of helplessness, a forlorn plea for somebody bigger to comfort her, take care of her, make it better.

It seemed to go on and on.

But after long minutes, the sound spent itself, and then she cried in huge, wrenching sobs that shook the bed. She clutched at the bedspread, wrapping it around her fists, pressing it against her eyes.

Finally, when the sobs lessened, she got to her feet, her knees almost buckling. In the bathroom, she vomited uncontrollably. When it was over, she sat on the edge of the bathtub for several minutes and stared at the blue tile before she could move herself to brush her teeth. Then she shucked off the damp jeans and t-shirt and stepped into the shower.

She stood motionlessly under the water steaming up around her in the glass cubicle as if it could wash away the horror that had been in the woods.

She needed Marian.

4

"Are you all right, Stef?"

The image that floated up was familiar, comforting. Chestnut hair cascading softly around Marian's face, a face lit by deep green-blue eyes. Marian Damiano, at thirty-four, was a strikingly attractive woman.

Stephanie rolled over, found a cigarette on the night table, and lit it. "I've been better."

"Did you find her?" There was a small silence. "Or was —"

"We found the body." Stephanie laughed shortly, humorlessly. "'Not a pretty picture,' as they say in the movies. I got back to the room just in time to have a slight breakdown."

"Why didn't you call, hon?"

"I didn't have a lot of time. It happened pretty fast. Besides, breakdowns cost more if you have them during long-distance calls."

"That's not really funny, you know."

Stephanie sighed and rubbed her hand across her eyes. "I know. It's lonely here. I feel like I'm hanging on by my fingernails."

"You want to tell me about it?"

Stephanie was silent for a moment. "No. Later. When I get home. What I want is for you to hold me so I'm not scared any more."

"Do you want to come home tonight? You could get a flight out of Atlanta and I could meet you in Jacksonville. We can get the car later."

"Marian, it's almost nine-thirty. There probably aren't any more flights out."

"If you leave in — " There was a small pause, as though she were looking for something. "If you leave in fifteen minutes, you can catch one at 10:55."

Stephanie smiled slightly. "I don't believe your efficiency sometimes."

"Well?"

"Well, I want to, but I can manage until tomorrow. Besides, you have classes in the morning. What are your students going to think if you fall asleep in the middle of Freud's theory of sexuality?"

"They wouldn't miss much," Marian laughed softly. There was another small silence before she spoke again. "Stef, are you staying because you think you have to deal with your feelings alone? That you have to be strong enough to make it by yourself?"

"Maybe that's a little of it."

"You don't have to, you know. You should be aware by now that you're not alone out there in the cold world, dear. Nobody gets good-conduct medals for suffering."

Stephanie smiled. "Is that the psychologist talking?"

"Maybe. And it's also someone who loves you. You put yourself through things that aren't necessary just because you think you have to be strong all the time. Well, maybe strength means leaning on somebody else once in a while."

"I don't like being afraid, Marian. I don't even like calling you now when I'm like this. What if you weren't there?"

"Stephanie, my love, if I recall correctly — stop me if I'm wrong

— but I believe you made it on your own for a number of years. Wasn't that enough?"

Stephanie felt the loneliness sucking at her again. She wanted Marian badly, wanted to be rocked to sleep in the warmth of her arms. But it was late, and there was really no need for her lover to drive the forty miles to Jacksonville when she didn't have to.

"No. I'll be okay. Really. I'll be home tomorrow."

"You're not answering my question."

"I know. God. Have I *no* secrets from you?"

"Probably not. But you *try* damned hard enough."

"Maybe that's why you've stayed with me so long. I'm a challenge."

"You really are putting distance there, aren't you?"

"*Yes.* Tomorrow. I promise I'll bare my soul to your psychological probing tomorrow. Tonight, I'll evade you with my fancy footwork. Okay?"

"With your wall, you mean." Marian sighed. "Okay. I suppose I can understand." She paused. "I'll be waiting for you," she said softly.

"I know. I count on that. More than I can say sometimes."

Stephanie could almost hear her smile.

"Yeah, I know you do. By the way, when do you think you'll be here?"

"I'm not sure. Early, I hope. If it's going to be after dark, I'll call."

"Okay. And Stef?"

"Yes?"

"Be careful. I worry about you."

When she hung up the phone, Stephanie leaned over, turned off the light, and pulled the blanket up. She yearned for the peace of sleep, but for a long time she lay in the darkness fighting off loneliness.

As a child, she had learned to pull an infinitely fragile curtain around her — "the wall," Marian called it. But it did protect her from the mental and emotional flood that sometimes threatened to inundate her — the wave of others' thoughts and feelings that could rise and break over her at almost any time.

The psychic vulnerability she had experienced as a child, the sensitivity that had bewildered and confused her, had grown over the years, and it would have been painful had her control not increased as well.

But the curtain that protected her often felt more like a cage that imprisoned her within its fine, crystal-sheer bars, preventing the closeness, the touching she really sought.

There were many who saw her power as a miraculous gift that lifted her above "ordinary people." She thought of it as a burden. She lived with it, used it hopefully for the benefit of those who came to her.

Except for that one time, came the mocking, time-worn thought. She pushed it down and felt it lodge like a heavy stone in the middle of her chest.

She did not embrace the power.

Now, as she lay alone, she felt unspeakably vulnerable. With exhaustion came the inability to draw the curtain.

Haunted faces hovered over her in the darkness, circled her in the chilly room. In the midst of them, Betty Jean Warren's eyes searched for her. Stephanie shivered under the blanket and tried to block the flood of memories.

And there was something else that coiled itself at the back of her mind: the growing certainty that Ray Dempsey was going to arrest the wrong man.

5

On the other side of Johnson, Dr. Michael Turner entered the county hospital's autopsy room and dressed for what he knew would be an ordeal. Dread for the operation squeezed his chest in a vise.

It was not the condition of the body, he thought. During his internship in Atlanta, he had seen almost everything. But it was always difficult when the victim was young. The waste of life was not something he thought he could ever harden himself to.

Shortly into the autopsy, he pressed back the tissues of the abdomen and had to force himself to continue. He reached into the gaping cavity and lifted the remains of a fetus from the tomb of its mother's body. His legs suddenly felt weak, and he leaned on the cold, stainless-steel table to support himself. For long minutes, he stared at the tiny lump of death.

Afterwards, he removed his gown and washed his hands for far longer than was necessary.

At home, he sat up with his wife in their bright yellow kitchen until it was close to three o'clock. They talked quietly while she nodded sympathetically now and then and caressed the back of his hand with her fingertips.

And in bed, he made love to her as though he were seeking his soul in the warm, inviting recesses of her body. When he failed to satisfy either her or himself, he laid his head on her breasts and cried, something he had not done in a long time. She cooed soothing words to him as if he were a child again. When he apologized, she stopped his lips with her fingers and cradled his head against her and told him how much she needed him to need her.

It helped him hold at bay the terrors of the night.

1984

1

Frank Talbot tilted back in the wooden swivel chair at Ray Dempsey's desk, his hands clasped behind his head, boots swung up on the corner of the old desk. From time to time, he shifted a toothpick from one side of his mouth to the other. His eyes were closed.

"Talbot. Get your goddamn feet off my desk."

He opened his eyes. Dempsey was pushing open the little gate in the railing that ringed the desk area.

Talbot scratched his chest where the checkered wool shirt itched. Then he slowly swung his feet to the scarred linoleum floor, stood up, and stretched. He knew it irritated Dempsey — that little delay before an order was carried out. He did it just enough to annoy Dempsey; never enough so he could really bitch.

Talbot smiled inwardly. Dempsey thought he ran the whole fucking town. But there was one man he couldn't run. Not ever.

"Where's Potter?" Dempsey demanded as he dropped heavily into the chair. It squeaked from its burden. He began rifling through papers in front of him.

Talbot lounged on the corner of the desk a few feet away and swung one foot back and forth so the heel of his boot banged the gray metal with a dull thud. The sheriff looked up. Talbot let his heel bang one more time and smiled.

"He's over at Decker's getting breakfast. Wanted me to watch things for a few minutes."

Dempsey scowled. "He's on duty."

"No problem, Sheriff. Glad to do it."

"Yeah," Dempsey said, his displeasure obvious. He looked back at the papers. "By the way, Talbot, half the town was in that search party last night. Where were you?"

Talbot shifted the toothpick and smiled. "Atlanta. Tell the truth, I didn't figure you'd be out looking till this morning. Besides, it looks like you had enough boys to do the job."

"So what're you doing here now? I thought you'd gotten that security job over at the mall."

Talbot folded his arms across his chest and shrugged. He could feel Dempsey watching him. The fat old fool would stare at him like that, not saying anything, and he'd feel himself starting to sweat.

"They can do without me for one day. I heard Danny turned himself in." It was okay; his voice was steady. Dempsey would never guess in a million years. "I figure he's gotta be scared, you know? He's just a kid. And things don't look so good for him right now. Thought he could use a friend."

Dempsey was still staring at him. He brushed a hand through his curly black hair and frowned. "Too bad about all this, huh?"

Dempsey studied Frank Talbot's face for a minute and leaned back in his chair.

Funny. Every time Talbot said something was too bad — in fact, any time a situation called for some feeling, Talbot just didn't seem to mean it. Like there was something behind his face that nobody could see. His eyes were as cold as ever.

"Yeah, it's too bad," Dempsey said sarcastically. "But it looks like it might not be over yet." He watched Talbot's eyes narrow slightly, then saw the smile that sprang back into place.

"You think maybe it was somebody else, Sheriff?"

The patronizing tone was clear; he might as well have added "you old fool" to the question.

"Well, we got all the evidence any jury'd ever need all right, but that psychic who's up here thinks maybe we got the wrong man. In fact, she'll be here later this morning. She called me before I left home." He paused. "I think we might have to take a mite closer look at this thing."

"Well," Talbot chuckled, "there ain't much chance of Danny not doing it, is there?"

Dempsey let his chair down with a thud. "There might not be a lotta chance in it, Frank, but I'm planning on keeping an open mind."

Something flickered across Talbot's face and left too quickly for Dempsey to catch.

"Well, I believe in keeping an open mind, too, Sheriff, but she could sure stir things up again, now couldn't she?"

"Maybe."

"What I mean is, she could make this town look awfully bad in the papers." His brow knitted in apparent concern. "And you'd come out looking pretty bad, too." The toothpick crossed to the other side of his mouth.

Talbot was wearing what Dempsey had come to think of as his sincere face, and it made Dempsey uneasy. It had even been that way when Frank was a kid. But he'd never known Talbot to do anything to prove those feelings right. Never. So, most of the time, he just didn't think about it. Just something in their personalities, he guessed. Some people rub you the wrong way, no matter what they do.

Dempsey probed at his stomach with blunt fingers. His ulcer was acting up again.

Talbot was still talking. "I mean, as long as Danny says he did it. And it was his knife and all." He paused, dropped his voice, and leaned over Dempsey's desk.

Dempsey resisted the urge to move away as Talbot's face came closer, his eyes almost glittering. It was a look he had seen over and over — the kind people got on their faces when they were gloating over somebody else's mistakes.

"You know, maybe he just got jealous," Talbot said. It was a voice that some men used when they were telling an obscene joke, Dempsey thought. When they believed other men felt the same way they did. "Everybody *knows* she was fucking practically every young stud in town, Sheriff."

Dempsey studied him, felt another twinge in his gut. He hated the coldness. And there was something else, too. Something he couldn't quite put his finger on. He sighed. Maybe he was just tired.

"Yeah, Talbot," he said. "I guess everybody knows she was doing that." He opened a desk drawer, pulled out a ring of keys and stood up. "I'll let you in to see Danny."

2

"Yeah, Danny, a man can do some pretty awful things during one of them blackouts."

Talbot shifted on the hard bunk and leaned forward, elbows resting on his knees, hands clasped lightly in front of him. The toothpick wobbled to the other side of his mouth. He knew he appeared relaxed, but he was resisting the impulse to throw the kid up against the wall and smash him in the middle of his big, stupid face.

Danny Alcott sagged on the bunk across the gray concrete cage and rubbed his blue-jeaned thighs as if comforting himself. Sandy-blond hair fell into his eyes, and he combed it back with his fingers in absent-minded habit. His eyes were dull, and he had been rambling on, making little sense.

There was nothing in the story Talbot didn't know already. Nothing at all. But he listened anyway and nodded in the right places so the kid would keep on talking, wouldn't leave out anything that had happened after he had awakened in the car on the cutoff.

Danny's voice had dropped so low that Talbot could scarcely hear him.

"And — and there was blood, Frank," he was saying. "On my shirt — and my hands..." His voice faded. He sat staring at the palms of his hands, then he turned them over to look at the backs.

Talbot leaned toward Danny and made his voice sympathetic. "Yeah, there'd be a lot of blood, you killing her in that way."

The young man's face screwed up, and he looked as if he might cry.

"You know, Frank, I really did care about Betty Jean." He sniffed and wiped his sleeve across his face. "I mean, I knowed what the other guys said about her, but I really thought maybe she was kinda lonesome. Like I was sometimes."

Talbot stifled a laugh. The biggest whore in town, and the kid had a soft spot for her. Well, it just proved he was stupid. Weak and stupid.

"You know, I was gonna come back to town and get the sheriff, Frank. But then I got to thinking that they might think I done it." His voice became a whisper again. "And — and then I got to thinking that maybe I *had* done it." He took a deep breath, and his shoulders trembled. "Doc said I was supposed to lay off the booze 'cause I had a couple of them blackouts a few months ago." His mouth twisted, and a low sob almost escaped before he regained control. "Well, maybe I done it for sure."

"It looks like it, Danny," Talbot said with soft intensity.

Danny nodded slightly. "So I — I dragged her out in the woods — and I left her there." The sob finally tore his throat, and he put his hands over his face.

Talbot smiled. The kid had told him everything he knew. Nothing he'd said could hurt Frank Talbot.

But, then again, Frank Talbot wasn't going to be stupid enough to figure the kid would remember everything. He knew enough about hypnosis and how people could forget things and then be made to remember them. Like part of their minds always knew what was going on.

And that bitch. Maybe she could look into Danny's mind somehow and see the rest of it.

So it was time to make sure that not even that other part of his mind could tell her anything. The kid was close to cracking anyway. It was going to be easy.

Talbot took the toothpick from his mouth and reached for a pack of cigarettes in his shirt pocket. Shaking one out, he lit it and leaned against the wall behind the bunk. The cigarette rested in the corner of his mouth, and he tilted his head to one side and squinted to avoid the smoke that curled up.

"You know, Danny, they say it don't take a long time to die that way, but it does."

Danny looked at him glassily. "What?"

"Remember that guy in Florida they had to shoot the juice through three times before he died?" Talbot's voice was soft.

An uncertain smile fluttered across Danny's mouth. He wiped

an arm across his wet eyes and stared at Talbot.

"And it hurts awful bad, Danny. Awful bad." His eyes held Danny's, and he began talking softly, steadily, in a voice that seemed to hold Danny Alcott in a dark web of terror. He seemed to know instinctively what would stimulate the fear, what would send the boy backing away toward the edge of a cliff that he would stumble over, out of Frank Talbot's life forever.

Soon, Danny started to shake all over. Talbot could feel the kid's fear, could smell it across the concrete cell. Sweat mingled with tears and ran down Danny's face, dripped off his chin, and he wiped a jerky arm across his face again. He breathed in heavy wheezes, seemed to be struggling for air.

Talbot's words hung in the air, almost tangible to him. He left them there for a while. He could *feel* them. He could almost see them. And he almost hated to see the words replaced by other ones. Ones that would set him free. He thought he could sit there for a long time and watch the fear.

Suddenly, while he was staring into Danny's eyes, an old, old memory flashed across Talbot's vision.

Out in the woods, he had found a raccoon caught in one of the steel traps his daddy kept set. Twelve-year-old Frank had sat down on a tree stump nearby and watched with morbid curiosity while the raccoon tried to free itself. It had looked at him as if it were pleading with the boy for its freedom — twisting, jerking in the cruel steel jaws that dug into its leg.

Finally, it had begun to gnaw on its own leg, making small, agonized whimpers the whole time. The boy sat there, his chin resting in his hands, watching the little animal until it had almost chewed through the bloody leg. It had taken a long time. Then he threw the burlap sack over it, released the trap, and bundled the raccoon home.

Now, as Talbot talked, he saw the look in Danny Alcott's eyes that he had seen that day in the raccoon's. Danny Alcott was looking at a death so horrible in his mind that Frank Talbot knew anything would be preferable to the fate he had painted for the young man.

"You know, Danny," Talbot said softly, "there's an easier way."

Danny's voice was hoarse, his face ashen-white, as if he were deathly ill. "What, Frank? What's an easier way?" He stared at Talbot as if he were looking at his salvation.

Talbot smiled gently at Danny, then he rose slowly from the bunk, not wanting to break the spell. He walked over to the sink and picked up the razor.

It was a metal one, the kind his old man had used before he died in that whore's bed in Atlanta.

Talbot felt the familiar, comforting rage gather in his gut. *They were all whores.*

He turned the handle, and the top rose, exposing the double-edged blade.

Danny watched with a strange fascination, his eyes riveted to the blade.

Talbot lifted it out carefully and stared at it for a long minute.

Then he slid it back in and screwed the handle down again.

"It could be much easier, Danny," he whispered.

3

Ray Dempsey showed Stephanie Nowland to a chair outside the railing and called over his shoulder, "Potter!"

A thin, red-haired young man stuck his head out of the door in back of the desk area.

"Bernie, get Alcott and put him in the interrogation room."

The deputy nodded, reached into the desk drawer, and pulled out a key ring. He strode down the corridor, his steel-tapped boots clacking on the concrete floor that began at the edge of the linoleum.

But he came loping back down the corridor too soon. He skidded to a stop at the railing and opened his mouth, but no sound came out. His face was pale, and he was breathing hard.

"Well, what is it, boy?"

"He's — he's—" The young deputy gulped and shook his head.

"He's dead," Stephanie said quietly.

The silence in the room grew until Stephanie could hear the two men swallowing hard.

4

Across the street, Talbot stood under the green-and-white striped awning of Decker's Cafe and lit another cigarette. His eyes were colder than usual.

Bitch. She could ruin everything for him. She wasn't supposed to be here this soon. If Danny hadn't done it right away, she still might get to him.

A siren screamed as an ambulance rounded the corner and screeched to a halt in front of the building that housed the sheriff's office. Two ambulance attendants disappeared into the building with a folded gurney and reappeared several minutes later, the gurney burdened now with a sheet-draped form.

Talbot stepped back into the alcove of the cafe's glass-doored entrance and wiped his sweaty palms on his jeans. He had to make sure it was the kid.

Shortly after the ambulance pulled away, siren silent, Ray Dempsey and Stephanie Nowland appeared. Dempsey patted her shoulder as she turned to get into the faded red Volkswagen at the curb. She seemed to hesitate a moment, a frown on her face. Talbot pressed himself against the wall and held his breath for a minute. Finally the car revved to life, idled for a minute, and then pulled away from the curb.

Talbot relaxed slightly and waited until he saw Dempsey disappear back into the building. He stubbed his cigarette out in the bedraggled potted plant beside the cafe entrance. The minutes dragged by.

Bernie Potter raced down the steps and up the other side of the street toward the newspaper office.

Talbot grinned with relief. Nobody else was in the place, so it had to be Danny. He chuckled, but he made sure his face showed appropriate concern as he crossed the street. Ten minutes later, he sauntered out and walked down to the corner, appearing to have nothing more on his mind than enjoying the warm spring morning.

But once out of sight, he jogged the three blocks to where he had left the white pickup. He hauled himself onto the seat.

She was staying! The filthy bitch was staying!

The cutoff.

What did they want out there?

He sat in the truck, his mind screaming, his palms sweating wet lines on the steering wheel. He slammed a fist on the dashboard.

Then he started the engine, made a U-turn in the middle of the block, and headed for Dotson's Motel. He drove slowly past the ten-unit brick building that sat near the center of town. The Volkswagen was parked in front of the motel, at the end of the building away from the adjoining restaurant.

A string of obscenities spilled over his lips. His rage and frustration rose to a manic pitch, and he shifted the gears in a grinding roar. His stomach was tangled in knots; his arms and shoulders were rock-hard with tension.

He braked to a jolting stop several blocks away and rested his forehead on the steering wheel. What was he going to do?

What?

He felt eyes staring at him, surrounding him, crowding him, seeking him out. His skin crawled, and the back of his neck tingled with the rise of near-panic.

Then, suddenly, a single thought cleared away the fear and confusion. His shoulders relaxed, his stomach became quiet, and he took a deep breath and let it out in a slow whistle. He sat up slowly, a smile creeping across his face. He rubbed his knuckles across his mouth.

He was going to kill her.

She really had given him no choice, he mused.

No choice at all.

He sat in the truck for a long time, savoring the thought, rolling it around in his mind, tasting it as if it were a sweet, intoxicating wine.

He caressed the polished handle of the knife folded in his pocket and grinned.

5

"Really. I'm okay. I'll only be here another day or two."

Marian shifted the receiver from one hand to the other to accommodate a fluffy orange ball of fur that had plopped itself on her lap and was purring loudly. She stroked the massive head that nudged her arm with loving insistence.

"That seems strangely familiar, my dear."

"Yes, I suppose it does, but—"

"Stephanie?"

"Mmm."

"I'm really concerned about you. You jumped into this thing too soon after that horrible business in Jacksonville, and it's taking its toll. Besides the mental and emotional drain, you're not eating well."

Stephanie started to protest, but Marian interrupted her.

"I *know* you. Grab a hamburger and Coke for lunch and then not eat anything until the next morning. And you're probably not sleeping."

Marian scratched Mr. Pye behind his ears. His startlingly brown eyes rolled back in his head as though he might swoon in his ecstasy. He had been named Pyewacket as a kitten, having arrived on their doorstep the day after she and Stephanie had watched *Bell, Book and Candle* on television. He had not looked like the witch's feline familiar in the movie, but the name had stuck nonetheless. When his true gender was discovered a couple of months later, however, the name was altered along with his future sexual lifestyle. As Marian had stated vehemently, Mr. Pye was not about to become a source of guilt for her every time a neighborhood cat produced a litter.

Now he turned himself around in her lap so he could gaze adoringly at her face. She smoothed his whiskers back.

"What you need is some decent food," Marian continued, "a couple of weeks on the beach with nothing to do — and your own bed. You'll be fine when you get home. I'm going to take the phone off the hook and *dare* you to put it back on for a week. I may *seem* like a piece of fluff, my dear, but you're going to find out just what a nag I can be."

There was no reply, and Marian said gently, "Stephanie?"

"I was sitting here wondering what I'd do without you."

"Well, that's not something you have to worry about — at least not any time soon. And when we get very old and a lot grayer, we'll make a pact to go at the same time or something." She smiled. "But for now, you need sleep."

"Well—"

"Promise?"

Stephanie sighed. "I promise to do what I can."

After Marian hung up the phone, she took Mr. Pye's head in her hands and stared into his eyes. He gazed back intently, as if he were listening carefully.

"Mr. Pye, Stephanie is going to be back very soon. Until then, we'll just have to do the best we can. Even though we worry about her. Okay?" She patted his head and laughed as he pushed his head against her chin. "Now," she said, placing him on the floor, "we've got work to do."

He padded after her into the bedroom, sprang onto the bed and stretched out, watching her.

Marian stood in front of the dresser and pulled out the top drawer. She began taking out flannel shirts, sweaters that would not be needed again for several months, and tossed them onto the bed.

As she went through each drawer, she noticed with a small smile the difference in the ways she and Stephanie kept their clothes. The drawers with her clothes were always cluttered, everything mixed together, even though they were neatly folded. But the half of the dresser Stephanie used was much tidier. Jeans and shorts stacked separately, shirts in orderly columns beside them. The arrangement of their clothes almost seemed to be analogous to the control they needed over their lives.

Stephanie had a deep-seated need for life to fit some logical, reasonable scheme, even though she constantly came into contact with the basic disorderliness of exsistence.

Marian, on the other hand, allowed her environment and the people in it to flow in and out, to interweave with each other in an apparent hodgepodge that she felt no need to arrange. Yet, her own life seemed relatively uncluttered compared to Stephanie's.

Perhaps it was Stephanie's need for things to make sense that kept her on the edge, Marian thought. It was difficult to make any sense out of violence. There were causes, certainly, and reasons for it that could be traced back through generations of families. Through eons of time, maybe.

But it never made any sense.

Their different ways of looking at the world had been obvious from the beginning. But she and Stephanie did seem to fit well together, regardless of the differences. Or, she considered, maybe because of them.

As she was about to close the last drawer, her eye was caught by the t-shirt on top of the pile, a dark-blue one that had begun to fray with age and wear. She smoothed her hand across it and smiled. It was the t-shirt Stephanie had worn that first night.

Finally, she closed the drawer. She looked at Mr. Pye on the bed and grinned as he stretched and yawned.

"Mr. Pye," she said, "I'm afraid I'm a hopeless romantic."

He closed his mouth and purred at her.

Part
Two

1980

Friday

19

December

1

"A psychic? You mean like a card reader? Fortuneteller? Christ, Karen, do you really think I've come to that?"

Dr. Karen Fowler laughed and patted Marian's hand. "No, no — nothing like that. Stephanie is just —" She shrugged. "She's just psychic."

Marian uttered a groan and took another sip of her bourbon-and-water.

The chattering hum and laughter of the party rose in tempo outside the library. She and Karen had escaped to its sanctuary when it became apparent that they would not be able to talk in the midst of the noise.

"Karen, why do you want to do this? You know I was just going to make an appearance — which you also know I rarely feel possessed to do — and you come up with this matchmaking attempt. I have the latest Stephen King thriller laid out on my bed next to my comfortable old flannel nightgown. And now you want me to give that up to meet somebody who'll probably want me to guess her sun sign and ramble on about the benefits of negative ions in the atmosphere." She stirred the drink with a finger. "Frankly, cocktail parties are bad enough, but this may put me right over the edge."

Karen laughed again, and Marian felt the corner of her own mouth twitch with a smile.

"Look," Karen said, "do you want me to tell you what I really think?"

"No. You're a great M.D., but I think you'd better leave the psychoanalyzing to husband Bob."

"He doesn't know you as well as I do. Besides, my Puerto Rican grandmother passed along a great deal of intuition to her favorite granddaughter."

Marian groaned again.

"You need to get out more," Karen persisted. "I think you and Stephanie would hit it off. As friends, if nothing else. She really isn't *weird* or anything."

"Karen, I've been working. Hard. If I don't get my doctorate now, it'll be a lot harder later. And that, along with my teaching schedule this semester, doesn't leave a lot of time for socializing."

"You have time tonight." Karen leaned back on the sofa, her slender body almost disappearing into the overstuffed cushions.

Karen's appearance, Marian knew, was deceptive. Beneath the fragile femininity that rippled the surface dwelt an iron maternal instinct that would eventually have its way. And also, she considered, Karen was probably right. Maybe she had been immersing herself too much in her work. It had been weeks since she had gone to a movie, visited friends. And if she were really honest with herself, she would have to admit that she was at least slightly curious about this woman who Karen was so insistent she meet.

"You're not going to give up, are you?" she asked Karen. "No."

"Look, how do you and Bob know her? I mean, I wasn't aware that your circle of friends included such esoteric people."

Karen smiled, obviously satisfied that she had finally managed to arouse Marian's interest.

"Well, Bob had a client who believed there was a negative spirit or something that was hanging around and wanted to harm her. Apparently she was afraid that when she went to sleep this spirit would kill her and she'd wake up in Never-never Land."

Marian frowned slightly, and Karen nodded her head.

"Mmm. It was serious. She couldn't sleep — except during states of severe exhaustion. She lost an enormous amount of weight, and the lack of sleep itself was promoting a psychotic condition. So Bob checked around and found out about Stephanie. He talked to her, and she seemed to have a level head on her shoulders. Frankly, he had some misgivings about it, but *he* wasn't getting anywhere with his client. It was a last-ditch effort."

There was a crash in the living room, and the laughter rose momentarily. Karen closed her eyes and shook her head.

"I'm really beginning to get over doing this every year. You'd think college professors and their spouses would be a little more civilized."

Marian grinned. "Alcohol seems to be a great equalizer."

"Yeah. Anyway, this woman went to see Stephanie just a couple of times and made what is called a 'remarkable recovery.' Whatever Stephanie did, she got through to her. Then the client went back into therapy with Bob. Afterwards, Bob and Stephanie became friends, and she and I met each other. We make it a point to get together as often as we can, but Stephanie's pretty much of a hermit herself."

Marian smiled wryly. "Like me?"

"Maybe. Anyway, I just want you two to meet. She *promised* me she would be here." She made a soft clucking sound of disapproval. "She was as hard to convince as you are. That alone should give you something to talk about."

Marian sighed. "Okay, you win. But I really am tired, Karen. Maybe I'll just stay here and curl up with my drink until she gets here. I'll be pleasant and smile a lot to please you, and then I'll leave."

Karen laughed and pushed herself out of the sofa. "Wonderful," she said. "That's all I ask."

Marian sank further into the sofa after Karen had left, pulled off her shoes, and propped her stockinged feet on the edge of the coffee table.

It had been a long time, she considered, perhaps five years, since anyone had done any serious matchmaking where she was concerned. Not since she had been introduced to Dave at a dinner party. And that had been enough for one lifetime, she thought.

The marriage had lasted two years — but it had only been good for one of those. At least the pain of separation had been less than the destructive pain they had visited on one another during the relationship. And they made much better friends than lovers.

She stood and wandered to the built-in floor-to-ceiling bookcases behind the sofa, bent over, and absent-mindedly looked over the collection.

The two affairs she had had with women since the marriage had been enough to convince her that her suspicions concerning her sexuality were correct. But she seemed to have a knack for attracting people who needed saving — whether male or female. She bandaged their emotional wounds, offered a loving ear for their problems, and fed them whatever nourishment, emotional and physical, they seemed to need. But so far, what she had also discovered was that when she had needed them, they simply were not there.

What she wanted was someone who was strong enough to be able to accept that caring and also to return it. And someone who wouldn't topple when *she* leaned.

The door opened, and the music and party noise grew louder until the door was closed again. She looked up.

A woman of perhaps medium height, several years older than herself, stood in the doorway gazing at her.

As Marian straightened, she took in the physical details. Dark eyes, short, dark hair brushed back in a soft, natural style. A thin, jagged scar that ran from just above the jawline to just below it. Body slightly on the lean side and relaxed, possessing an easy grace, Marian sensed. Hands shoved deeply into the pockets of soft gray slacks, a white tailored blouse opened at the throat.

But it was really the eyes, Marian thought. It was the penetrating gaze that captured her in that first instant. She opened her mouth to speak and found herself incapable of uttering any sound at all.

A wave of warmth engulfed her, and she felt very suddenly as if the woman standing in the room with her was taking her in, *holding* her in some inexplicable way, *flowing* around her, *surrounding* her. She began to feel as if she were floating in that warmth. Her knees seemed weak.

And then, whether a few seconds had passed or it had been a much longer time, Marian began to sense that she was *known* to this woman — as if her entire life, her secrets, her thoughts and feelings were open to this woman. She gasped softly as she realized with a suddeness that seemed to take her breath away that she was standing naked and exposed before the woman. She became acutely aware of the way her softly clinging dress hugged her hips, teased her ribcage, caressed her breasts. Her skin was feverish, tender, sensitive. She could feel — in that brief instant that seemed to stretch for an eternity in back and in front of her — she could *feel* this woman's hands caressing her naked body, feel her mouth seeking out the warmth of her responses. As if this woman knew already what would create her small cries of pleasure, knew she would respond intensely to a gentle firmness, even to a sweetly rough lovemaking at times, knew how to turn her into a surrendering, loving animal.

And Marian began to hunger for the touch of this woman's hands, her mouth.

But then, just as she thought her knees might fail to hold her on her feet for one second longer, the feeling — the spell, really — was broken. The room swam back into focus, and she heard the noise outside the library. Her cheeks suffused with heat, and she knew her face had flushed pink.

The woman moved toward her across the room and extended her hand.

"Ms. Damiano, I presume," she said, a slight smile touching her mouth.

And Marian held out her own hand and smiled shakily in return. But it did not escape her notice that the dark eyes that met her own were gently apologetic.

Neither of them, she knew, would deny what had happened.

"Non-alcoholic," Karen whispered as Stephanie dipped frothy punch into three glass cups. "I'm afraid some of our guests are more than a little tipsy. But they'll never know the difference. They'll think vodka's in it."

When Karen had left in response to a guest's leave-taking wave, Marian said quietly, "I don't think her obvious pleasure with herself has much to do with the punch."

Stephanie laughed softly. "No. I doubt it." She handed Marian a cup and held her eyes for a moment. "I didn't mean to do that to you in the library."

Marian studied her for a few seconds before she spoke. There seemed to be a trace of sadness in the dark eyes.

"Then you—"

·49·

"Yes. It wasn't just you." Stephanie reached into the pocket of her slacks and drew out a cigarette case. Tapping a cigarette on the edge, she said, "I'm sorry. I wasn't expecting that to happen. Once it started, I found it difficult to stop."

Marian watched as the case was tucked back into the pocket. Strong, competent hands, she thought. Strong, gentle, loving hands that could — She stopped herself abruptly, pulled herself back from the brink of melting once more.

But as Stephanie brought the lighter up, Marian took it from her and held it in her own hand, feeling the warmth it had absorbed from Stephanie's body. Then she thumbed the wheel. The flame burst into life, and she moved it to the tip of the cigarette, aware of Stephanie's eyes on her, aware of the question is those dark eyes. She closed the lighter quietly, let it rest in the palm of her hand and watched as Stephanie gently lifted it out. Her hand was left open, vulnerable. She smiled slightly and dropped her hand to her side.

"I'm not entirely sure I like my response to you."

"You're not sure you like it," Stephanie questioned softly, "or you're afraid of it?"

Marian met her eyes. "I am afraid of it."

Stephanie looked away, and again there seemed to be a hint of sadness in her expression. But when she turned back, she said, "Will you see me again?"

Marian was silent for a long minute before she responded. "I feel very vulnerable right now. I want to run away. And I want to stay." She paused. "I need a day or two to think about it."

Stephanie nodded. "Yes," she said. "All the time you need."

2

At one o'clock, unable to sleep, Marian finally turned on the lamp on the bedside table and picked up a book. After she read the first paragraph perhaps five times, she slammed the book back down on the table and turned off the light.

Her body again felt sensitive, the skin almost painfully tender. She stretched under the sheet. She had taken off the nightgown an hour ago, and her hand had drifted down over her stomach several times since, but she found she was unable to touch herself, unable to give herself the physical relief she needed. For some inexplicable reason, she did not want the relief — unless it came from Stephanie Nowland.

She gritted her teeth in irritation at herself. This whole thing was beginning to sound like some goddamn romance novel. She was a self-sufficient human being. She would *not* give in to this *madness*, she told herself. With a groan, she turned over and studied the telephone. It was insane. It was one o'clock in the morning. She was acting like a child. She punched a fist into her pillow and threw her head back onto the bed again.

At two-thirty she was still awake, her body aching. She stared at the wall where the luminous clock dial cast a glow, then looked at the telephone again. Finally, with a soft "Damn," she picked up the receiver.

There was only one ring before Stephanie answered. Marian closed her eyes, pulling the warm voice around her.

"I'm sorry to wake you."

"I wasn't asleep. I'm glad you called."

"You know what I'm going through, don't you?"

The voice was gentle. "Yes. I think so."

"It's ridiculous."

"Is it?"

"I feel like I should be protecting myself." Marian laughed softly. "I guess the truth is that I don't really want to, or I wouldn't be calling you." She paused. "I don't need to, do I?"

There was a silence.

"I think you know the answer to that."

Marian nodded silently. She did know the answer. She had known it all along. "I want you," she murmured.

"Yes. I know."

There was another, longer silence before Stephanie spoke again. "Do you want me to come to your place?"

Marian said nothing for a minute.

"Marian, do you need me to tell you in words how much I want you? Do you really need to hear it after what happened?"

Marian shook her head slightly. "No. It's enough just to know that you do."

"And you do know."

Marian uttered a soft cry; she felt her resistance melting. Something that had slept inside of her for years was awakening. A need, a longing that she had pushed away many times, fearing it might be used against her. She wanted this woman to take her in a very old-fashioned, romantic sense of the word — to possess her completely. It was a yearning in her body that seemed to overwhelm her with its intensity. And there had never been anyone before whom she had trusted with that much of herself. She allowed its stirrings now, and as she spoke, her voice trembled.

"Stephanie, I want to be in *your* bed."

In the silence that followed, she felt that Stephanie was listening before she answered.

"Yes," Stephanie said gently. "I understand."

And Marian knew she did.

When Marian pulled into the driveway in front of the house that sat back among the palm trees, she leaned her head on the steering wheel. Now that she was here, she felt again the need to protect herself, to hold back. What if she were wrong about Stephanie? She had only just met her a few hours ago. She knew nothing about her, she—

The screen door squeaked open, and she watched as Stephanie, dressed now in jeans and a dark-blue t-shirt, her hair looking just-combed, came toward her. As she reached the car, she placed her hands on the opened window and leaned down. Her forehead was creased with a frown of concern. Her voice was low, and it seemed to Marian that it enfolded her, held her in caring arms.

"Come into the house. We can talk — just talk — if you want to."

Marian nodded, and Stephanie opened the door so she could slide out. But as she stood, she took Stephanie's hand and felt its warmth, its strength. The last of her resistance seemed to slip away so quietly that she could hardly remember it had been there.

"I don't want to talk," she said softly. "I want you to make love to me."

When Marian returned from the bathroom, Stephanie was in bed, the sheet lightly covering her body. A candle glowed on the table beside the bed, creating a soft aura in the room.

Marian began to undress, but the intensity of Stephanie's eyes was disconcerting, and she hesitated.

"Do you want me to look away?"

Marian gazed at her lying on the bed, the naked arm bent under the dark hair, the gentle, questioning frown. It took several seconds before she realized that she did not want Stephanie to look away. She did not want her to do that at all, she thought.

"No," she said quietly, "I want you to watch."

And her undressing then had been for the woman who was watching her with such intense eyes.

She unbuttoned her blouse slowly and slipped it off her shoulders, aware of her full breasts as they were exposed in the soft light. She unzipped her jeans, acutely aware of Stephanie's eyes taking her in, holding her, caressing her nakedness. And as she slipped the jeans and then her panties over her hips and down her legs and bent to remove them, it had all been for Stephanie.

And she knew that Stephanie knew it.

As she slid between the cool sheets, warm arms went around her and pulled her close. She gasped as she was pressed against Stephanie's body, felt the strong hands touching her. She shivered as these hands slid down her back, cupped her buttocks firmly, and drew her even closer.

Then, without warning, her body was trembling uncontrollably.

"I feel like I'm losing myself," she whispered.

"Maybe," Stephanie murmured, "it's just the letting go."

Marian searched the dark eyes for the reassurance she needed, saw the tenderness in them — and the wanting. And for once, she knew she could let go.

For at least this one time, she did not have to fear the letting go.

And with a soft moan, she gave herself to the loving.

"For someone who talks so easily about letting go, you seem to hold on awfully well."

"Sometimes it's — necessary." Stephanie smiled slightly. "I spent a long time developing self-control. It seems to have overlapped into other parts of my life." She frowned. "But you knew you satisfied me, didn't you?"

Marian laughed softly and traced a finger around the curve of Stephanie's mouth. "Oh, yes, my dear. I could tell. You were just very quiet about it. Not like your friend here, who was acting like a truly depraved woman."

"I enjoyed the way you were."

Marian grinned. "I'll just bet you did."

She traced the thin scar across her firm jaw. "What happened?"

Stephanie's eyes went darker, and she reached over to the table and found a cigarette. "It happened a long time ago," she said. She lit the cigarette and put the lighter back on the table. "A very long time ago." She smiled and met Marian's eyes. "I have a feeling that I'll probably tell you about it very soon."

"But not now."

"Not now."

There was a long silence as Stephanie smoked the cigarette, Marian curled in the crook of her arm. Finally, when the cigarette was near its end, Marian looked at her again.

"Stef?"

Stephanie glanced at her and smiled. "Nobody has ever called me that before."

"Do you mind?"

"No, I like it."

Marian snuggled closer. "Stef, are you lonely?"

There was a long silence.

"Sometimes."

Marian moved the ashtray to the table, took the cigarette from Stephanie's fingers and crushed it out. Then she shifted so she was holding Stephanie in her arms. After a few minutes, she felt the trembling of the slender body, and she knew the loneliness was more than just "sometimes."

After Marian had gone to sleep, Stephanie lay on her side, feeling Marian curled up beside her.

What happened? Marian had asked.

And as the curtains across the windows lightened with dawn, Stephanie remembered the fear and the pain of that day.

Her fingers prying into the little girl's mind. The scream that seemed to go on and on as the fear was squeezed. The terror that twisted the little girl's face.

Her sister's face.

The blood that tinged the edge of the knife in a shining ribbon. The blood that ran down her own face.

The fact that she had been a child herself at the time had never made any difference to her, had never lessened the guilt she had shouldered.

The fact that no one had ever believed that she had viciously attacked her own sister, driven her into a black well of insanity, had never made any difference.

Stephanie pushed at the ache that had lodged itself in the middle of her chest. Each time it returned, it seemed to implant itself more firmly, became harder to dislodge.

Stephanie disentangled herself and turned over. She pulled Marian close and held her as she awakened, the deep blue-green eyes unfocused at first. A slow smile began as she realized where she was.

"Are you too sleepy?" Stephanie asked.

"Mmm?" Marian brushed hair out of her eyes and back over her ear. "For what?" she mumbled.

Stephanie smiled. "What I had in mind was breakfast."

Marian planted a small kiss under Stephanie's ear. "That depends," she said, "on what's on the menu."

Stephanie felt Marian's mouth curve into a warm smile against her ear, and she laughed softly.

The ache retreated again.

Part
Three

1984

1

As Stephanie Nowland tossed fitfully on the bed in the darkened motel room, Frank Talbot sat in his truck on the side street that dead-ended in front of the motel. From time to time, he dragged raggedly on a cigarette.

His visibility was beginning to make him jumpy. He was going to have to make a move in the next couple of hours. She was due to meet Dempsey out at the cutoff at noon, and it was already close to ten o'clock.

He started the truck, rolled to the corner, took a jog to the right and then to the left, and came to a halt on the side street beside the motel. Her room was on the end of the building next to the street. The restaurant was attached to the other end.

It should be easy.

Flicking the cigarette out the window, he stared at the building. He would park the truck a few blocks away and walk back. Then he frowned. If he were seen, it might be more reasonable for the truck to be nearby. He could always lie about why he was there. Maybe he could say —

Then, quite suddenly, the frown disappeared. In its place a smile sprang out. He laughed softly and rubbed his knuckles across his mouth.

Two teenaged girls huddled over ice cream sodas in the first booth as Talbot walked into the motel restaurant. No one else was there except Harry, who was scraping grease off the grill behind the counter.

Talbot slid into the booth closest to the back, near the door that led to the restrooms and the exit door, and glanced out the window to his left. No other cars were in the motel parking lot — just the one the bitch was driving.

It was perfect.

Rose would be sitting in her little kitchen now in the apartment behind the motel office — feeding her face probably. And even if she saw him skirting the back of the building, he'd let her know she'd better keep her mouth shut good like she had for the past six months. She wouldn't give a shit what happened to Frank Talbot, but she knew if Buck ever found out about those little afternoon jollies, there would be hell to pay. At least for Rose. Buck was smart enough to know not to touch Frank Talbot, no matter how he felt about it.

Talbot chuckled. It was perfect. Just perfect.

He called to Harry for a cup of coffee. Harry was going to be added insurance.

2

Unable to sleep, Stephanie got up, feeling more exhausted than before. She opened the curtains across the window facing the street.

Dogwoods had burst into life, azaleas puffed into gigantic pink and red balls, and rich yellow buttercups marched across well-manicured lawns up and down the street. She shuddered. It was a pretty facade that hid the ugly reality.

Death was a dark-brown copperhead that slithered among the magnolias.

Two-story, white frame houses built in the nineteenth century lined the maple-shaded main street like sentinals of the community's morals. She could almost hear the clucking behind the imposing, solid-oak doors.

Betty Jean Warren was a tramp, the whisperers would say. *Always had been. Too bad, really, but she was bound to come to no good end. Always hanging around the boys, never did have any girlfriends. No wonder. No decent girl would have anything to do with her. And did you know she was pregnant?*, they would whisper, hands half covering their mouths as they bore the "shameful" secret. *Her mother didn't even know, you know.*

They would ignore the reasons for Betty Jean's "loose morals," would refuse to understand the need for love that drove her into encounters that left her emptier each time. No, they wouldn't see that as they passed their dirty stories over their luncheons on the verandahs and took them out of their lunchpails down at the factory.

Of course, Danny had been a little wild lately, they would recollect. *Not a bad boy, really, just a little wild. And, after all, he was a man — bound to get what he could if she'd let him have it. Probably tried to get him to marry her and he just flew off the handle. Seems I remember him being right much of a hot-head sometimes.*

They would rock on their porches in the cool dark, satisfied looks on their faces, the fireflies glimmering among the shadowy elms. They would sip in the gossip with a brandy or gulp it down with a cold beer, a few more lights turned on this evening to keep the darkness away.

And they wouldn't say it out loud — it might be thought uncharitable — but in their warm, safe beds that night, some of them would think, *She deserved it.*

Now, they would have Danny Alcott to feed on, too. Stephanie's mouth compressed into a grim line. They would do a thorough job of it.

An image festering in her mind since a long-ago vacation to the Keys sprang out at her from some dark, dank-smelling cavern.

A desolate highway invades the Everglades wilderness between Miami and Key Largo.

On a muggy, stifling-hot afternoon, a small, hapless animal had been crunched under the wheels of a killing machine on the shimmering highway that runs through the scrub palmettos and brush. Stephanie and Marian had seen a huge, shifting mound of brown in the distance, heat waves rising from the road making it difficult to see until they were almost upon it.

Careening buzzards had become a macabre flock of satisfied mourners at the funeral, feeding on death to sustain life.

Stephanie had leaned on the horn, a raucous noisemaker in the middle of the silence, and the carrion-eaters had taken slow, lumbering flight. But she saw them settle heavily in the trees, and she knew they would just wait until the silence closed in again.

And there were people in this small town who would feed on Betty Jean Warren and Danny Alcott until they had picked the bones clean.

She felt sick again — as sick as when she had seen the blood dripping from the beak of one of the huge, prehistoric-looking birds they had passed.

The guilt sprang out at her from an adjacent cave.

She rubbed her eyes and sighed. *She* had given them Danny Alcott to feed on. She had led them to him. If she had not told Dempsey about the knife, Danny would be alive now. Knowing that Ray Dempsey would have sought out Danny eventually — or that the young man had turned himself in — did not alleviate the crushing weight of her guilt.

The old, heavy stone settled itself in the middle of her chest.

3

Frank Talbot motioned for the white-haired man to sit opposite him as Harry Suttles slid the coffee cup across the table and plopped a sweet roll on a napkin beside the cup. He heaved his bulk into the booth, his huge stomach brushing the table.

"Whatcha know, you ol' bastard?" Suttles rasped.

Talbot smiled, poured cream out of the tiny plastic container into his coffee, and stirred the swirls into a rich brown.

"Well, Harry, I was just wondering if Rose was home."

Suttles shook his head and grinned. "I tell you, Frank, you gonna get your balls shot off one of these here days. You just asking for it, buddy." He leaned over the table and stabbed a meaty finger into the faded-pink formica.

"Now you listen to what I'm saying, you mothafucker. Buck is gonna come home one day, find that blond-haired piece sucking you off, and it'll be the end of your screwing days for *sure*." He leaned back in the booth and laughed boisterously, his belly bouncing under the grease-splotched white apron.

The girls whispered and giggled at the cash register, and Suttles pulled himself out of the booth with a groan.

"Yeah, she's home, Frank." He winked broadly. "Give her one for me, huh?" He laughed all the way to the counter.

Talbot grinned and slurped the hot coffee. The sugary roll melted in his mouth. Now, if *anybody* saw him, Harry would believe "good ol' Frank" was just getting a piece of ass like he always did.

It was goddamned perfect.

He licked the sugar off his fingers and smiled as he looked out the window toward the motel.

4

Stephanie closed the curtains and went back to the nighttable for a cigarette. As she lit it, she was aware of something still playing at the edge of her mind. It had been there since she had stood with Ray Dempsey outside his office.

It was a sensing akin to waking up at night, lying in bed with the darkness all around you, and smelling something burning. You try to remember if you turned off the oven, wonder if someone could have dumped smoldering ashes into a wastebasket, and you finally get up to look for it.

The sensing was malevolent in its elusiveness. She shook her head. She simply could not pinpoint where it was coming from nor even what it was. After a few minutes, she picked up the telephone and called Ray Dempsey.

As she left the motel, she did not see Frank Talbot staring at her from the window of the restaurant, disbelief and rage clouding his face.

5

Stephanie squinted and lifted her hand to shade her eyes against the sun. She had read somewhere that the sun's rays in April were as fierce as in August, due to its position. It didn't feel as hot because the atmosphere had not yet warmed up, or the rays hit the earth at a slant, or. . .

She shook her head in irritation. If she could concentrate, perhaps she could give the sheriff information he could use to find Betty Jean's killer.

Bernie Potter sat in the shade on the right side of the road that wound up to the creek. A fair-skinned redhead, he had begun to look decidedly pink after only an hour. Dempsey stood in the road a short distance away, facing the spot where they had found the body.

Stephanie had hoped she could find some bit of evidence, something that had escaped her attention the night before. She also had hoped it would be a simple matter, but time dragged by, and only this vague sense of dread persisted. She took a deep breath, let it out slowly and stood quite still, reluctant to open herself to the evil that lingered in this place.

That was really the problem, of course. She did not *want* to open herself to it again.

There had been too much lately, Marian had said.

In Jacksonville, seven elderly women had been raped and murdered in their homes over a period of a month. After several haunted nights of sleep in which their killer stalked them in her dreams, Stephanie had called the police and offered her assistance.

She seldomly initiated the contact. It was difficult enough to move through an atmosphere of death and fear without also having to confront the smirks of those who thought they would look foolish if they cooperated with her, or the stony stares of those who resented her stepping into a case they might have been trying to solve for weeks — and seeing her solve it.

And, of course, there were always those who were simply afraid — some because they equated her ability with the supernatural, others because they were afraid she would discover their vices along with the killer.

And there had been the crank calls in the middle of the night: those who wanted to quote passages from their Bibles when their own private demons disturbed their sleep — their evidence proving she was a tool of satanic forces, if not a demon herself. Theirs was a god of justice and revenge — never love. In their god, there was no room for differences. And they believed whole-heartedly that they were doing that god's will.

Stephanie's real difficulty with the callers, though, was that she could *feel* their panic, their life-constricting need to do what they thought was right. Her heart went out to their minds; she spoke soothing words. And they lashed out at her even more vehemently, fearing she was trying to suck them into some maelstrom of evil.

Always before, the cases had taken her far enough from home to lessen the intrusion. The callers wanted to save her eternal soul, but few of them wanted to do "the Lord's work" if it entailed an expensive telephone call.

In Jacksonville, they had been too close.

One who had crossed that fine line of insanity had shown up on her doorstep while she was in a counseling session with Mrs. Berkley. Stephanie had forgotten to put the small sign on the front door, and Marian had been in the backyard.

When Stephanie opened the door, a man in his twenties, clothed in a rumpled, musty-smelling suit, confronted her. His eyes were a little too bright, she had thought. His hair was greasy and limp, and he smelled as if he had not bathed for several days. He did not look like one of those whose clothes and neatly combed hair hid the fanaticism — his appearance more closely matched his mental state than was usually the case.

When she refused his demand to enter the house, he clutched at her, his dirty, cracked fingernails digging into her arm. He shouted meaningless phrases at her, wildly shaking a finger in her face.

His emotions flooded her open mind, her body, like a tidal wave, suffocating her. He pinned her against the door and harangued at her while she tried in desperation to close herself off from him.

Marian came running around the side of the house then, pulling off her dirt-caked gardening gloves. She tugged the little man onto the porch, threatening to call the police. He scurried down the driveway, hysterically screaming back over his shoulder about the fire and damnation that awaited them.

By that time, Mrs. Berkley had appeared in the doorway leading to Stephanie's small office and was wringing her hands anxiously. Stephanie composed herself enough to accompany the elderly woman to her car and give her a reassuring hug before she drove off.

But it had taken the rest of the day for Stephanie to shake off the violence of the attack. She *knew* it was ridiculous to allow the abuse to affect her that deeply, but it was as if her emotions, her gut reaction to the incident — and others like it — refused to be quelled by any intellectual reasoning.

Now, in Johnson, Georgia, she shook her head and kicked at a piece of gravel in the road. Her mind was wandering again. And all her thoughts were black. Not *every* person in this town was enjoying the misfortune of Betty Jean and Danny, she knew. Not *every* person she met in her work was full of malice toward her. In fact, there were probably very few of either. But her depression seemed to color everything right now.

She sighed heavily and crossed to the left side of the road, away from where the body had been found. After a moment, as she walked along the top of the embankment, she felt a subtle pull to her left. She stopped and eyed the ditch at the bottom of the embankment, then began walking again, more slowly. After a couple of yards, the tug subsided. She turned, walked back, and in a few feet, she felt the pull again, heavier now.

Puzzled, she looked into the tangle of dead limbs and brush on the other side of the ditch. She glanced up the road toward the sheriff, then back into the brush.

It might be nothing.

She half-slid down the slight embankment, scattering gravel with her. As she came to a jarring halt at the bottom, Dempsey turned and jogged down the road. He slid awkwardly down the embankment after her.

"Something here?"

Stephanie frowned. "Maybe."

As she peered into the underbrush, sunlight glinted off an object. She pointed, and Dempsey pushed his way into the thick tangle, holding back branches as he pressed forward, stepping carefully over dead limbs. Stephanie wondered at his ginger progress until she remembered that the area was probably infested with snakes. She shivered slightly. She was not particularly afraid of snakes in general, but copperheads and coral snakes were another matter.

Dempsey bent down and tugged at a limb. He reached into his back pocket, shook out a large white handkerchief and stuck his hand back into the tangle. He lifted out a pint whiskey bottle by the top, touching as little of it as possible.

Potter stood at the top of the embankment now, his red hair flaming in the sun. He put out a hand for Stephanie, and she scrambled up the bank.

The sheriff started to hand the bottle up to Bernie, but when the young deputy reached for it, Dempsey snatched it back and shook his head. "Bernie?"

"Yeah, Ray?"

"You know what I got this handkerchief around this here bottle for?"

A puzzled frown crossed Bernie's forehead, then he smiled broadly. He reached into his back pocket, but his hand came out empty.

Dempsey stared at Bernie and shook his head again. Stephanie turned her head so Bernie would not see the slight smile. She liked him; he was sweet, she thought. But, as Marian would say, he was no "intellectual whiz."

The sheriff leaned against the embankment and laid the bottle on the road. He stabbed a finger at Bernie. "Don't touch that." Bernie nodded. Dempsey slowly made his way up the slope, waving off Bernie's outstretched hand.

When Dempsey reached the road, the three of them stood silently, staring at the bottle.

Finally, stooping down, Stephanie looked up at the sheriff. "I'm going to have to touch it. If I'm in contact, I can get a clearer picture."

Dempsey nodded, ignoring Bernie's hurt expression.

Stephanie stood still, the top and bottom of the bottle resting between her palms. The sensing grew heavier. It drifted around her, still elusive but at least stronger. She closed her eyes and cocked her head to one side, as if she were listening.

After several minutes, she heard Bernie and the sheriff fidget slightly, heard the gravel shift under their feet. A light breeze stirred her hair across her forehead. She deepened her concentration until she entered a dreamlike state, her energy totally centered on the object in her hands. She frowned. Everything was so dark. Then she realized that she was not viewing the darkness from outside. She was in the midst of it.

Danny Alcott slumped in the front seat of the car parked behind the tavern. The jukebox tune drifted faintly in the still air.

Then a dark figure shoved a whimpering Betty Jean into the back seat of the car, cracked a hard hand across her face, yanked the dress up to her waist, and beat a fist against her slender thigh when she protested.

The knife flashed.

The dark figure was behind the wheel.

But his face was in the shadows. She could not see him.

She let go then, surrendered to the darkness, to the sensing so completely that she seemed to be in the dream herself.

She was standing on the steps of the building that housed the sheriff's office.

The dream-self turned languidly to get into the car, as if in a slow-motion nightmare, and she stared across the street toward the row of stores. A café with a green-and-white awning sheltering the doorway.

A dark figure — a shadow — stood next to the door.

The shadow moved and stepped into the glaring white sunlight.

She felt swallowed up by the sense of evil that clothed him, the cloak of chilling madness.

Black curly hair glinted in the sunlight.

An icy smile crawled across the hard, thin mouth.

The checkered western shirt, the jeans, the scuffed boots.

Fighting for control over her fear, Stephanie pushed herself far enough toward consciousness that she could speak.

Her mouth was dry. She swallowed hard. Her voice was a rusty, hushed monotone in the quiet of the road as she described the man she saw.

Afterwards, she bobbed up to full awareness and opened her eyes. Her hands were trembling, her knees felt weak.

Bernie was staring at Dempsey, his mouth open. The sheriff was looking down the road, frowning.

"Ray," Bernie gulped, "that sure sounds like — like Frank, don't it?"

Dempsey rubbed at his eyes in weariness. "Shut up, Bernie," he said softly.

After a long minute, he turned toward her, and she saw in his eyes a dull anger.

"Bernie's right, Stephanie. Who you're describing is Frank Talbot."

He stared down the road again.

"Frank Talbot is one of my deputies."

1984

1

As Stephanie drove into downtown Saint Augustine, the four-hundred-year-old Castillo de San Marcos loomed on her left. It squatted on a slight rise overlooking Matanzas Bay, a massive fort constructed of coquina, a kind of shell-rock. Erected by the Spanish to protect their territory from the British and French, it had never been breached; the town of Saint Augustine had stood under Spanish rule until it had been given over to the British in a treaty.

In a sense, it symbolized to Stephanie the solidity of her life in "the oldest city" for the past ten years — years that had almost stilled the pain of those that had come before.

The damp sea air washed off the bay and engulfed her, and she inhaled deeply, savoring the fragrance. It was a fishy, salty odor — a smell of the primeval, perhaps.

It was the sea.

For some reason she had never been able to fathom, it seemed to move, to live in the furthermost corner of her soul. It healed her when nothing else could touch her.

Coming back to Saint Augustine was like returning to a lover who always waited for her.

Stephanie stopped for the traffic light a couple of blocks past the fort and gazed to her left at the Bridge of Lions spanning the bay. The water glowed warmly in the late-evening sun under the bridge. Guarded by huge white stone lions, it crossed the bay created by the

Matanzas River and gave way to the road that led onto Anastasia Island and Saint Augustine Beach.

Just past the bridge and to her right, across parallel Charlotte Street, sat the Plaza, a village square that sat behind the Old Market. Once the center of the old town, where settlers exchanged news and bought fresh produce when it was available, it had become a landmark surrounded by shops, the Cathedral of St. Augustine, and, on an adjacent corner, a movie theater and the famous tourist attraction, Potter's Wax Museum. On the wax museum's old corner, facing the bridge, was now Dolls in Wonderland, a museum of antique dolls.

Giving Dolls in Wonderland only a perfunctory glance as she passed it, Stephanie continued down Avenida Menendez, the continuation of San Marco Avenue as it passed the old fort, and followed the Matanzas River until she left it to enter a much quieter section of the city.

Minutes later, Stephanie pulled into the driveway of the green-shingled house at the end of the cul-de-sac. Its yard seemed to be a well-managed jungle these days — since Marian had moved in with her three years ago. Ferns proliferated, the oleander trees were pregnant with pink blossoms that would burst out soon, small palms were scattered among the larger ones.

Marian was bent over, digging in the caladiums again.

Stephanie smiled. Marian never seemed able to let the yard alone. Either she was tending the flowers, pruning the oleanders, spreading mulch or rooting up the weeds as if they were her mortal enemies.

The earth, Stephanie thought — green, growing things — was Marian's sea.

Marian straightened from her work, and a smile spread across her mouth. She walked toward the car, smoothing out long strands of hair with the back of her hand.

Stephanie grinned at her, and Marian's stride broke slightly, just a trace of hesitation in the middle of a long-legged step, as if she were suddenly, acutely aware of Stephanie's eyes on her — aware of her full breasts cradled in the halter top, her ample hips moving within the shorts, her thighs touching each other warmly. She stuck her head in the car window and pressed her mouth against Stephanie's for a long moment.

"I've missed you — and the way you look at me," she said when she pulled back.

"And I've missed you," Stephanie said softly, touching Marian's warm, damp cheek with her fingertips. "But what *are* the neighbors going to think of this?"

"Darling, if they don't know by now, they are either blind or stupid."

Stephanie laughed and pulled Marian's head down and kissed her again, savoring her fragrance.

When Marian finally pulled away, she was smiling languidly. "It has been a *long* time."

Just then, Mr. Pye appeared at the corner of the house. He trotted across the lawn and sat at Marian's feet, staring up at her.

Marian laughed and picked him up, and he turned to look at Stephanie with liquid brown eyes. He strained toward her, and when Marian held him close to the window, he nuzzled the side of Stephanie's neck until she stroked his head. As Stephanie opened the car door to get out, he plastered himself against Marian's chest and placed his huge paws on her shoulder. Within seconds, he had pushed his head against her ear to purr into her hair.

"He really does think you're his mother, you know," Stephanie laughed.

"Mmm. Well, his mother has other ideas about who she wants to take care of right now." She looked at Stephanie for a few seconds, then put her arm around her waist. Her voice was soft. "And we've got plenty of time for it."

2

Ray Dempsey sat at the scarred wooden desk, turning a pencil end over end. He grimaced and pressed his fingers to his stomach for what seemed to be the hundreth time that day.

Down the corridor, Talbot had been silent all day. Last night, he had raged in the cell for hours. The screaming had gone on until Talbot's voice grew hoarse, and then he had started banging things on the bars. Dempsey had tried to handle the problem by taking away anything that made noise, but Talbot had merely beat his fists on the walls then.

After Talbot had managed to dislocate three knuckles, Mike Turner advised Dempsey to put up with the noise. He had given Talbot a tranquilizer, but it had taken the doctor, Potter and the sheriff to hold him down for the injection. And Turner had gotten a black eye for his trouble.

Dempsey decided it was easier to deal with the commotion than go through that again.

But even after the tranquilizer had worn off, Talbot had been quiet. Dempsey had walked back to see him, and he had been sitting on the bunk, staring at the floor, softly muttering obscenities to himself. Dempsey had felt a chill crawl up his spine.

Once, when he had first become a deputy, before old John Banner had died, Dempsey had visited the state mental institution, where he had seen a man who reminded him of Talbot. The man seemed to be caged up in his head, Dempsey had thought, like he was running around in his head screaming and slamming doors up there. Sometime later, Dempsey had read about the man in the newspaper.

The staff had considered him to be cured. He was quiet, well-behaved, smiling.

And they had let him out.

The next day, the quiet, well-behaved, smiling man had gone home, cut his wife into little bloody pieces and left a piece on the doorstep of each house in the neighborhood.

And Talbot. He had seen Talbot with that smile that looked like he'd picked it up and put it on when he walked in the door and then took it off when you turned your back.

Somewhere, deep inside, Frank Talbot was cold. He was flirting with madness down there in that cold spot, Dempsey thought.

It was a kind of craziness that could look fine on the outside — the kind that could hide the rotting smell of death behind a smile.

And those feelings he'd had about Talbot all these years. He had pushed them back time and again. Maybe he could have done something more. After all, he had known Talbot's history. The mother who had run away from the beatings delivered by Frank's father. The father who had poisoned his boy's mind from the beginning. And that father's own death at the hands of a jealous husband. It was a lot for a kid to take without it twisting his mind.

Dempsey grimaced again and burped. He reached into the desk drawer and dug out a bottle of Tums. As he popped two into his mouth, he considered that he could at least get some sleep tonight. He had been up all last night, he and Sam Breck. Tonight, things had settled down enough so he could leave Potter.

There was something about leaving Bernie with Talbot that made him a little nervous, but the boy was scheduled to work, and he couldn't be coddled forever. Just as long as Talbot had his supper and Bernie had a phone number to call in case of trouble, he should do okay.

Tomorrow, the Georgia Bureau of Investigation would send a man down from Atlanta. Right now, Dempsey was holding Talbot on evidence that wasn't going to hold any water at all. But the GBI would be able to find what they needed to get Talbot convicted by a jury.

Dempsey knew Talbot had done it. All he needed was hard, concrete proof.

3

Later that night, Frank Talbot sat on the bunk in the cell and stared at the concrete wall opposite him. His hand throbbed even through the pain-killer. But sometime this afternoon, he had finally gotten control of the rage that was eating away at his guts. It was still there, but he had managed to push it down far enough so he could think — had pushed it down far enough to figure out how he was going to get out of the hole the bitch had dropped him into yesterday.

It had to be tonight.

While Bernie was here.

Tomorrow would be too late. Once the GBI agents got here, it was going to be all over. He knew their methods. Knew they would find him out. They could find the evidence Dempsey wanted without hardly trying. They would put everything under a fine-toothed comb, put everything under their fucking microscopes, use chemicals, anything. Footprints alongside the parking lot where he'd scuffled with Betty Jean. One of her hairs maybe in his shirt.

He could explain away most of it. But there would be too much after they were done.

They would find him out.

They would know everything.

He stood and called down the corridor. "Hey, Bernie! Got a cigarette?"

Bernie came loping down the hall. At the cell, he stopped and shifted from one foot to the other and smiled hesitantly.

"Sure, Frank. The sheriff says you can have one whenever you want." He avoided Talbot's eyes. "But he says I gotta stand here while you smoke, and I'm supposed to light it for you."

Talbot smiled at him, and Bernie smiled back. Every time the stupid asshole gave him a cigarette, he said the same thing. Even though he had been arrested for murder, Bernie still wanted his "old buddy" to like him. Shit, the kid wanted everybody to like him.

"That's okay, Bernie. I know Ray's making you do it." He watched as the young deputy ineptly lit the cigarette and shook out the match as if he were afraid of it.

Talbot sat on the bunk and smoked the cigarette slowly, savoring the harsh taste. He glanced at Bernie standing in the corridor, his thumbs hooked in his gunbelt.

"By the way, buddy, you know if you want to take a nap, you could just leave the smokes and matches here. That way, you wouldn't have to bother with running down here every half hour. And you know I wouldn't tell him, don't you?"

Bernie shuffled his feet and rubbed his hand across his mouth. "Well, Frank, I can't do that. I'm sorry—"

"But Bernie, what can I do with them? I mean, Ray is trying to do what he thinks is best, but you know he's getting a little old. He's just not thinking very clearly. He's being *too* careful." He laughed. "I sure can't kill myself with smokes, can I? And I sure as hell can't break out of here with them." He patted the steel bars gingerly with his bandaged left hand. Even out of control, he had instinctively damaged the hand he used less.

"Well, I guess he—"

"It really wouldn't hurt, now would it, Bernie pal?"

Bernie frowned and rubbed his mouth again. "I can't do it, Frank."

Talbot's voice grew soft, almost seductive. "Bernie? You remember that time you was supposed to be locking up that drunk, and you turned your back, and I got him just before he scrammed out the door?"

Bernie nodded, a sheepish look crossing his face.

"Well, do you suppose," Talbot said, staring at the tip of the cigarette, "that Ray might want to know about that?"

Bernie frowned. "You wouldn't tell him, would you, Frank? I mean, I just turned my back for a second — just to get the keys."

"No, Bernie," Talbot said, looking up at him again. "I won't tell him. Not if you leave the smokes. I'll give them back before he gets in tomorrow morning."

Bernie shuffled his feet anxiously. But, finally, he stuck the cigarettes and matches through the bars. "Now, Frank, you promise to give them back before he gets here? He'll be awful mad at me if you don't."

"Sure, buddy," Talbot said. "I promise."

Bernie turned and walked back down the corridor. When he was out of sight, Talbot pressed his head against the bars and listened intently until he heard the squeak of the chair.

Quickly, he turned and tugged the mattress off one corner of the steel-latticed frame. He struck a match against the pack and watched as the flame shot up, then he held it under the corner of the mattress, where it smoldered briefly. A small orange flame leaped up in a few seconds. When it had become a strong blaze, he went to the bars and yelled down the corridor.

Bernie came trotting back to the cell. By that time, the flames were raging around the mattress, and his mouth flew open as he stared at the thick smoke that poured toward the ceiling and was rapidly filling the cell.

"Omigod, Frank! What—"

"Bernie! Get the keys!" Talbot screamed. "I'm gonna die in here!"

Bernie spun, slipped on the floor, righted himself, and charged back down the corridor.

Talbot squatted near the floor to avoid the smoke that billowed from the mattress. He jerked his shirttail out and held it over his nose and mouth.

He chuckled softly.

It was goddamned perfect.

But that was before Dempsey appeared in front of the bars, his hat spotted from the light rain that had begun falling outside. The shotgun in his hands was pointed at Talbot's head.

Bernie shuffled his feet nervously and kept his eyes on the sheriff.

"Get the bastard out, Bernie," Dempsey said quietly.

1984

Friday

11

May

Stephanie was staring out the kitchen window, the paring knife poised over a carrot, when Marian walked in.

"Hey, lady! I thought you'd have all this done by now so I could sit back and relax!" She took a bottle of milk from the refrigerator and glanced at Stephanie.

"What's going on, honey? You look like you're floating around with both oars out of the water."

Stephanie started peeling the carrot again. "I don't know, I don't seem to be able to shake it."

"I thought it was all over, Stef." She took the carrot from Stephanie and nibbled on it as she leaned against the counter. "He's been locked up for two weeks now, and they're bound to get a conviction."

"Well, that's not it. I keep thinking that if I hadn't told Dempsey about the knife, Danny Alcott would still be alive."

Marian studied her for a minute. "Too bad you're not perfect," she said quietly.

"What does that mean?"

"It means, it's too goddamned bad you're not perfect. It's too bad you can't see what consequence is going to result from every action you take."

Marian reached into the cabinet for a glass, avoiding Stephanie's cool gaze.

"Think about it, Stef. What you're saying is that you should have known what was going to happen when you told the sheriff where the knife was. You should have known that Danny Alcott was going to turn himself in. You should have known that he was going to kill himself. And you should have known from the beginning who really killed her."

She poured milk into the glass. "Forget the fact that you were falling apart yourself and probably shouldn't have even been there."

"Look, I—"

"No." She set the glass down on the counter with a bang; milk sloshed over the rim. "I've been keeping this in way too long. You've got this power to see things. And you think that it means you should be saving humanity. But you're human yourself! Christ, Stephanie—"

Stephanie turned away. When she spoke again, her voice was as cool as her eyes had been. "I'm glad to know what you think. So it's your considered opinion that I should be doing nothing."

"No! For God's sake, Stef, you have to do what you *can*." She reached out to touch Stephanie's arm, hesitated, then dropped her hand to her side. "What I'm trying to say is that most people bitch about how bad things are and then leave it to somebody else to clean up the mess. You're not like that, and it makes you pretty damned valuable."

She paused and rubbed a hand across her forehead. "But you've got to stop taking everything on yourself. You can let other people be human, make mistakes, but you can't tolerate it in yourself. Everybody else gets your sympathy, your understanding. Everybody but you."

Stephanie stood stiffly, still staring out the window.

"You're not God, Stef. You didn't kill that seventeen-year-old girl. You didn't arrest that kid for doing it. And you didn't kill him, either. You did what you could. And you can't keep on blaming yourself for everything that everybody else does. Don't punish yourself with guilt about what you have no control over—"

Stephanie turned when she heard the catch in Marian's voice, but Marian had looked away, her face wet with tears.

"I'm sorry, Stef. I get scared sometimes. I think some day I'm going to pick up the phone while you're gone, and they're going to tell me some maniac killed you."

Stephanie reached out and touched her arm, but Marian pulled away. "No, please don't touch me. If you do, I'll never be able to finish." She looked at Stephanie and wiped her face with her hands, then she folded her arms across her chest.

"It took me too long to find you. I don't want to lose you now." She looked down at the floor. "And it's not only that. Ever since you've been back, even when we make love, you're not really with me. And I feel hurt about that."

Stephanie reached for her again and held her through the brief resistance Marian put up. Then, with a small cry, Marian released her arms and put them around Stephanie's neck. She sobbed against her shoulder while Stephanie held her.

"Don't you know," she whispered against Marian's hair, "that I'm afraid, too? Not of being killed, but of losing you. All I want to do is to hold you. But it's so hard sometimes to open up, to be that vulnerable. I can't do it with anyone but you, and sometimes it's even hard with you. I'm so used to closing myself off, to not feeling. And I'm afraid you'll leave me if I show you how helpless I really feel so much of the time. I'm afraid to hold you as tightly as I want to, so I push you away."

Then, so slowly, so subtly that she could not say when it happened, Stephanie began to feel Marian's breasts pressed against her. She felt Marian's back arch slightly as she caressed it, felt the long length of thigh move against her own. She heard the small intake of breath, and Marian's hands began caressing her gently at first, then insistently. She felt Marian's breath warm against her ear, her voice low and husky.

"Make love to me, Stef. Now. Please. Like you mean it."

Stephanie pulled away from her, trembling, took her hand and led her down the hall and into the bedroom.

She fumbled with the catch on Marian's halter before it came loose, and in the half-darkened room, Marian's breasts spilled out, the nipples already hard. She cupped one in her hand, feeling its silkiness and warmth, and bent her head to take the nipple into her mouth. She felt Marian clasp her head gently between her hands and heard the quickening of breath.

Stephanie eased the jeans over Marian's hips, and Marian bent to step out of them. Stephanie caressed the smooth, strong back, feeling her own breath coming more rapidly now. Marian leaned against her, her arms around her neck, but as Stephanie slid her hands up Marian's back again, Marian drew away slightly to unbutton Stephanie's shirt. Stephanie stopped her, her voice hoarse with a desire that surprised both of them.

"Lay down," she whispered.

Then, as she drew off her own jeans and shirt, for the first time since she had come home, she completely surrendered to her need for the closeness, the touching. She wanted Marian desperately, wanted to feel her heated, sensuous body moving under her hands, wanted to give her pleasure, wanted Marian's response to move through her own body. Her need for the touching was so intense that it was painful.

She lay down beside Marian and pulled her close, kissing her hungrily, exploring her mouth and biting at her lower lip. Marian's eyes fluttered open once, nearly unfocused, and she reached to touch Stephanie's breast. Stephanie gasped at the touch, but as Marian's hand moved further down her body, she whispered, "No. Don't think about me right now."

Marian smiled and closed her eyes again. "Yes," she murmured, "anything you want."

Stephanie's hands caressed Marian's body then, teasingly gentle with her one minute and firm the next, bringing her to a sweet moaning and then a small cry, until Marian's body was trembling hard. Until Marian was moaning softly, steadily, deeply in her throat. She clutched at Stephanie's back then, her breathing ragged. She spoke haltingly, her voice harsh.

"Please, honey," she breathed, the words almost a cry of pain. "Now. Please."

And several seconds later, as Marian's back arched and she cried out, her hands clenched by her sides now, Stephanie lowered her mouth and hungrily caught Marian's cry in her own throat.

Afterwards, her body bathed in a fine sheen of perspiration, Marian laughed softly. Her eyes shone in the dim light that filtered through the curtains. "I'd say that was worth waiting for."

Stephanie smiled, and Marian reached to kiss the corner of Stephanie's mouth, the hollow of her throat.

"Now you," Marian whispered.

This time, Stephanie did not stop her.

1985

Frank Talbot lay on the bunk in the concrete-and-steel cell at Reidsville State Prison and stared at the smoke that curled from his cigarette toward the bare light bulb hanging from the ceiling.

Just thinking about her seemed to still his mind.

It made it easier to get through the endless days of boredom. It kept his temper in check when he wanted to smash a guard in the face or tear the fucker's eyes out because he looked at him like Frank Talbot was some kind of bug the fat slob could crush under his foot.

He toyed with her in his mind to keep himself from going stir-crazy.

He played a macabre game with her to keep from doing hard time.

But one day, it would no longer be a game just in his mind. And when that day came, he would destroy her the way she had destroyed him.

He would take a long, long time with her.

In the end, she would kneel at his feet, lick his boots, and beg him to kill her.

The bitch was going to *beg* him.

He took a deep drag, blew the smoke at the light bulb, and grinned.

Part
Four

1988

Sunday

3

July

Ricky Blanchard reached over and scooted the pointer on the radio down the lighted dial once more. Nothing but static greeted his efforts.

He shook his head and slapped his face a couple of times. It was two in the morning, and if he didn't get coffee soon, he was going to go under. He should have stopped on his way out of Atlanta, but he had been too excited then to think about how he was going to stay awake. A little hot coffee and some No-Doz, and he'd be able to make it for two more hours.

He drummed his fingers on the steering wheel. Why in hell did Mary have to go up to her mother's when she was eight months pregnant? Of course, there didn't really seem to be any reason for her not to go. The doctor had said she was in fine health, no reason to worry. She'd be back home in plenty of time for a normal, safe delivery. But the doctor hadn't counted on her taking a spill in the back yard while she was playing with her nephew.

When her mother called a little over an hour ago, though, she had reassured him. The hospital said Mary was okay; it was just that the fall had put her into labor early.

Ricky smiled suddenly then as he thought about why he was heading for Birmingham in the middle of the night.

Mary. The *baby*.

He chortled and whooped out loud into the cool blackness. Maybe he would get there before the baby was born. He pressed his foot a little harder on the accelerator.

A huge lighted sign glared beside the interstate from a truck stop. Pulling in, he got a large cup of coffee to go and purchased a small box of No-Doz on his way out. A few minutes later, he emerged from the restaurant into the startlingly bright parking lot, slid under the wheel and opened the steaming black coffee.

Twenty miles further west on Interstate 20, he heard the shuffling noise in the back seat. He explained it away as the wind shifting something around back there.

But when the hand touched his shoulder, he felt his scalp crawl.

1988

Wednesday

13

July

1

She was being chased down an infinitely long, black tunnel. Harsh breathing followed her; she could feel it on the back of her neck — hot, fetid, a nauseatingly rotten odor. Scrabbling, bony fingers clutched at her shoulder, slowing her headlong flight. She fought for each breath, the dry air burning her lungs. Her heart pounded at the wall of her chest. Her legs pumped, aching.

No matter how fast she ran, it was still behind her, toying with her. An evil, dark laugh echoed in her ears.

Stephanie bolted upright in bed, gasping. Perspiration bathed her naked body; the sheet was tangled around her legs.

Quickly, she released herself from the sheet and slid out of bed. She stood and took long, shuddering breaths, trying to calm herself. She felt her way around the bed, toward the door, not wanting to awaken Marian. Fumbling blindly for her robe on the chair, she found it and shrugged it on.

In the living room, she opened the door onto the porch and stepped outside. It had just rained, and she took huge gulps of fresh, damp air.

She ran her hands through her hair and stared out into the yard for several minutes, frowning. Finally, she sat in the swing on the far side of the porch, leaned back, and closed her eyes.

The screen door squeaked. Marian stood in the doorway, her nude body silvery in the moonlight that slivered through the palm fronds in the front yard. Her voice was sleepy soft.

"What are you doing, honey? It must be three or four o'clock."

"Four-thirty." Stephanie patted the swing beside her. "Come and sit down."

"I thought you liked my bottom more than that. There're probably a million splinters there."

Stephanie laughed softly. "Well, if you didn't run around like a naked wanton, you wouldn't have to worry about it."

Marian grimaced at her, disappeared into the house, and came out again belting a terrycloth robe. She sat down and leaned against Stephanie.

"It's been a long time since this happened. Is something wrong?"

"I don't know. Just a dream."

"A nightmare?"

"I woke up and couldn't breathe. I was scared."

"What about?"

Stephanie sighed heavily. "It feels like there's somebody out there — waiting."

"Who?"

"Well, it might just be the dream, but I keep thinking about that man in Johnson."

"You mean Georgia?" Marian frowned. "That was — God, it would have to be four years ago. He'll be in prison for years."

"I know."

"Don't you think the sheriff up there would've let you know if he'd been released?"

"I suppose so. If he knew."

"Well, maybe you should put your mind at rest about it. Call and make sure the guy is still locked up."

Stephanie sighed. "I suppose you're right."

Marian pushed herself out of the swing, turned, and held her hands out to Stephanie. When Stephanie stood, Marian put an arm around her.

"Good. Now how about if we go out and get breakfast and then go for a walk on the beach. We can watch the sun come up. It'll be late enough then so you can make the call." She hooked her arm through Stephanie's. "And afterwards—"

"Mmm? Afterwards? You have something in mind?"

Marian lifted her eyebrows in a pretense of naivete. "Well, we probably need to get a little more sleep, don't you think?"

Stephanie smiled slightly. "You know, I thought that after all these years you'd get tired of me."

"Tired of you? Did you really think that?"

Stephanie shrugged, feeling a little embarassed. "I guess it's my background. I always had the idea my parents were never particularly sexual. At least they never showed it much. I suppose I got the idea that after a while, in any relationship, sex became non-existent."

"Mmm." Marian opened the screen door. "Well, my dear, my background is truly different. If we kids didn't see my dad pinch my mom's bottom at least once a week, we assumed they were fighting."

Stephanie stopped halfway in the door and grinned. "Really? In front of you?"

"Indeed," Marian said emphatically and pulled Stephanie through the door. "And don't forget how much like my mother I am."

Stephanie laughed and shut the door behind them.

2

It was after eight o'clock when Stephanie hung up the telephone in the living room. She frowned and wandered into the kitchen, where Marian was making a pot of hot tea. Mr. Pye was hunched over a bowl beside the refrigerator, crunching dry cat food.

"Well, it looks as if you were right," Stephanie said as she opened the refrigerator door. Mr. Pye looked up at her, gave a brief purr, and turned his attention to the bowl once more.

"Oh, what did he say?"

Stephanie found a lemon and set it on the counter. "He escaped a couple of weeks ago."

"*Escaped?* That hardly sounds like I was right."

"Apparently he headed for Mexico." She took a knife from the holder on the wall and started to cut the lemon. "He broke into a small clothing store in Atlanta and stole several pairs of pants, shirts, things like that, along with a few dollars. They found his prison clothes in a trashbarrel outside. They assume he hitchhiked into Alabama."

She arranged the slices on a saucer. "He stole a car out on I-20 — near Anniston, I think. He shot the driver—"

She saw Marian's grimace. "No, he didn't kill him. He rolled him into a ditch along the interstate, apparently thinking he was dead. The description the man gave matched Talbot's. They found the car later behind a grocery store in Baton Rouge. It was a few blocks from the police station."

"The *police* station?"

"Yes. It does seem a little strange, doesn't it? The car he picked up in Baton Rouge was found in Houston. There were a couple of prints on it. From there, they lost the trail." Stephanie placed the saucer on the table and went to the cabinet for mugs.

"So maybe," Marian said, "you just sensed he was loose again."

"It looks like it. But just in case it turns out differently, Dempsey gave me the name of a detective on the police force here. Gary Achison."

Marian studied her. "So he's on his way to Mexico, but if we happen to see him, we get it taken care of right away. So what's the frown about?"

"Well, I keep thinking that he left an awfully clear trail."

Marian placed the teapot on the table. "What do you think it means?"

"Think about it. The clothes outside the store, which were a dead giveaway. The man he shot — who didn't die even though he was shot at close range—"

Marian nodded. "The fingerprints on the next car."

"Exactly. It was like dropping bread crumbs all the way to Texas."

"Then nothing."

"Right."

"So he took the Houston car to Mexico."

"It seems logical." Stephanie reached for the teapot and filled her mug. Marian pushed her own mug across the corner of the table and Stephanie filled it and pushed it back before she spoke again. "The problem is that Frank Talbot impressed me as the kind of man who wouldn't make those mistakes. He made a lot when he killed the girl in Johnson, but he wouldn't do it again. He would have made sure that man was dead so he couldn't talk. He would have worn gloves so he wouldn't leave prints."

"Maybe he wasn't thinking clearly," Marian said. "He was scared. Or — with what you've said about him — maybe he was thumbing his nose at the cops."

"I don't know." Stephanie took a careful sip of the steaming jasmine tea.

"What are you thinking?"

Stephanie was silent. He probably *was* in Mexico, she considered. That he would be after revenge four years later — particularly that he would be after revenge on her when there were so many others who had helped put him in prison — was perhaps farfetched. It was much more reasonable to assume that his objective was to get out of the country as fast as possible and that he had made mistakes along the way. Or that he wanted to put one over on the police.

And the nightmare — it was just her sensing that he was loose again.

She shook her head, smiled, and reached across the table to pat Marian's hand. "You know my imagination sometimes. Right now, he's probably throwing back margaritas in some little village in Mexico, congratulating himself."

"Paul — Felker, wasn't it?"

"You've got a good memory. The first time I was in here was last night."

Manuel Cendoya set the frosted glass of beer on the black-topped bar in front of him, picked up a cloth under the counter, and started running it over the bar. He smiled amiably. "Well, my friend, I try to remember faces and names. But yours wasn't too hard."

"Yeah?" The voice was hard.

"The beard and the moustache." The look that was shot at Manuel from behind the thick-rimmed glasses was icy. "I mean," he hesitated, "it's a little like mine, don't you think?"

The customer continued to stare at him.

"Look, I hope I didn't say something to offend you, my friend." He was silent for a minute, and he felt uncomfortable under the steady gaze. "You from up there? North?"

"Everything's north from here, ain't it?"

Manuel chuckled. "Sí. You are right."

"No. I'm not from around here."

Manuel waited, his face smiling expectantly, but nothing else seemed to be forthcoming. The smile began to feel heavy on his face. He looked down at the bar. "So what you doing down here?"

The stranger took another gulp of the cold beer, then his eyes stared piercingly at Manuel again.

"You got something else to do?"

Manuel was transfixed by the stare for long seconds, and he felt a sudden chill on the back of his neck. He took a short, involuntary step backwards, as though his feet no longer belonged to him. He looked away and swallowed. He felt his throat muscles work hard, as though he were trying to get down an especially large, sharp chunk of fear.

"Sure thing," he said quickly, and his voice sounded weak in the dimness of the bar. "You don't wanna talk, then it's no talk."

"That's good." The stranger's voice was soft, but there was menace in it. "Real good." Then he shook a cigarette out of the pack in front of him and tapped it on the bar, his eyes still on Manuel.

Manuel sidled away down the bar, leaned over and began washing glasses in the hot soapy water. He concentrated on being as quiet as possible.

When he was alone again, he straightened from the sink, wiped his hands and forearms on the bar towel. He picked up the bills on the bar, rang the sale on the register, and shoved the tip into a pocket under his apron. He continued to watch the door while he cleaned the ashtray with a damp cloth already covered with black smudges.

Manuel Cendoya, he thought, was a big man. He could throw out drunks with one hand tied behind his back if he had to. And here he was backing down like a boy with a runny nose from an hombre maybe half his size.

He had been afraid of this one. There was a knot of fear in his gut that was only now beginning to disappear. The place was icy cold, yet his armpits were spreading big circles of sweat on his shirt.

It was the smile, he thought, putting the ashtray back on the bar. Like some animal was sitting behind that smile, waiting.

Just waiting.

He moved to the end of the bar and looked out the window for a minute. Then he ran down the shades that shut off his view of the old Spanish fort across Matanzas Bay.

1988

1

"Go on and say it."

"No. I refuse. I don't like to fight in the morning."

"Goddamn it, Stephanie, I can see it in your eyes. Say it."

Stephanie sighed and put the bag of groceries down on the front porch while Marian fumbled in the huge beach bag that doubled as her everyday handbag during the summer.

"Okay," Stephanie said, her eyes closed tightly. "I surrender." She took a deep breath. "I cannot *believe* that you carry that thing around!" She shoved her hand into the beach bag. "It's no wonder you can't ever find anything. We could go away for the weekend on an impulse, and we wouldn't have to pack anything. We could just take this bag." She pulled out a bottle of shampoo.

Marian grabbed it from her, stuffed it into the bag again, and continued to rummage through it. She laughed and slapped Stephanie's hand in the bag. "There are things in here I *need.*"

"Of course," Stephanie responded, her eyes rolling upward. "Like a bottle of five hundred aspirins, three packs of cigarettes—"

"They're *your* cigarettes!"

"It is *not* necessary to carry three packs of *my* cigarettes at all times, dear. I am fully capable of providing my own vices."

"I guess I'm afraid you'll run out and I'll have a raving lunatic on my hands."

"*And,*" Stephanie said, digging into the bag, "I hardly think it's necessary to carry two-year-old mints and a half-eaten package of peanut-butter crackers."

Marian swatted Stephanie's hand again. "You never — ever — can tell," she said solemnly, "when you'll be stranded on a desert island." She paused and gave Stephanie a mock-fierce look. "*And* — when *you* have to carry it, *you* get to decide what to put in it!"

Stephanie backed away, a grin spreading across her face. "You're right. Absolutely right."

Finally Marian found the key and held it up in a gesture of triumph. She handed it to Stephanie, who mumbled something under her breath.

"What?"

Stephanie smiled at her innocently. "Nothing — nothing at all." She moved Marian gently to the side of the door and inserted the key into the lock.

As the door swung open, she reached down and picked up the bag of groceries at her feet. Straightening, she stared into the living room, her body suddenly stiff.

"What's wrong?"

When Stephanie did not answer, Marian moved into the doorway. She gasped and dropped the beach bag.

Stephanie reached out a hand to her, but Marian had moved back several steps, her face pale.

Stephanie forced herself to look back into the room. The windows were open, as they had been left an hour before. The curtains, pushed back to let light into the room, fluttered in the warm breeze. It was a light, airy room, simplistic in its furnishings, decorated with framed prints they both loved. It had been a room they had enjoyed.

But now, in the middle of the room, on the fine oak coffee table left to Marian by her grandmother, sat Mr. Pye's head, neatly severed at the neck, eyes gouged out, in a spreading pool of dark blood. The blood had run over the top of the table, made thin streams down the sides, and dripped onto the Oriental carpet.

The body had been opened from neck to tail and was draped like a bloody, orange-furred rug over the back of the sofa. The entrails had been scooped out and spread over what seemed to be everything in the room. The odor of stomach contents and feces was overpowering.

Stephanie fought a wave of nausea and turned back to Marian, who was trembling violently, her breath coming in hard gasps, her hands twisted in front of her. Stephanie moved shakily to the swing and pulled Marian after her, pushing her gently into the swing. Stephanie struggled with her own feelings, felt her heart racing, knew her hands would tremble if she held them in front of her.

Finally, Marian took a shuddering breath and wiped her hand across her eyes. She took Stephanie's hand and squeezed it hard. "What monster could do that? What *reason* could anyone have to do it?"

Stephanie ran her hand through her hair. Suddenly, she felt old, incredibly tired. She looked toward the doorway.

"He's telling me he's here."

2

It was early afternoon before Stephanie pushed open the back screen door and stepped onto the stoop. Marian stood in the corner of the yard across from the vegetable garden and stared at the green plastic bag that lay beside the mound of dirt she had thrown from the grave.

As Stephanie walked toward Marian, a light breeze wafted off the inlet that ran beyond the yard on the other side of the live oak woods and down a hill. But, strangely, the smell of the sea and the bay did not have its usual effect on her. In fact, for a split second, it seemed to overwhelm her, to deliver a sickening blow to her stomach. She took a deep breath, though, and the effect was gone. Puzzled, she frowned slightly.

As she reached Marian, she took the shovel and made the hole deeper while Marian looked on, silent. Neither of them spoke until the bag had been placed carefully into the hole and the earth was tamped down again.

"I was going to plant roses here," Marian said. "I guess I still will."

"That would be pretty."

Marian nodded and then looked away.

Stephanie turned and placed her hands on Marian's shoulders. "I'm sorry about Mr. Pye. I mean, not just because he's dead, but because he wouldn't be dead if—"

"Stéphanie, stop it," Marian said gently. "You didn't do this, sweetheart, and I will not tolerate your feeling guilty about it. Besides, I'd have to share at least half of the guilt, because I said I thought that maniac was in Mexico, too. And I refuse to feel guilty. There's nothing we could've done about it."

Stephanie nodded and picked up the shovel, then they began walking back toward the house.

"What are the police going to do?" Marian asked.

"There's nothing they can do."

"He's an escaped murderer!"

"Well, in the first place, Frank Talbot is considered to be three thousand miles away. Gary Achison will be coming by again tomorrow, though. At least he seems willing to listen."

"I assume they didn't find any fingerprints."

"Nothing."

Marian sighed. "So what's left?"

"Not much, unless we can convince Achison that it *is* Talbot. If not, then as far as the police are concerned, there's very little they can do. Whoever did it has not threatened *us*. There was no message, no phone call, nothing. The only thing they could even charge him with — if they found him, which is highly unlikely — is criminal trespassing and—"

"*Trespassing?*"

"The window was open, so breaking and entering is out. Nothing was taken, so there was no burglary. He killed an animal and destroyed private property. Not exactly crimes they can spare half the police force on."

"Since they assume it's not Talbot."

"Right."

"So what are we going to do?"

Stephanie leaned the shovel against the house beside the steps. "I don't know yet. I guess first we'll see what Achison can do."

"You're an admirable product of your Italian heritage."

"I know. Food solves all problems. Eat."

Stephanie lifted a thick slice of ham from the platter Marian had pushed in front of her and added it to her plate. She ate a little of it, then forked a piece of broccoli. She chewed and swallowed before she spoke.

"There's only one thing we *can* do now."

"If you suggest that we just wait here so he can walk in and slaughter us, I'll outvote you." Marian put down the slice of tomato she was lifting to her mouth. "God. I'm sorry. I'm getting macabre."

Stephanie eyed her carefully. "Are you all right?"

"I will be."

"We can talk later."

"No. Tell me what you're thinking."

Stephanie pushed the half-full plate away and lit a cigarette. Marian grimaced as Stephanie pulled an ashtray toward herself.

"Well, at least Achison believes us. So he'll get Talbot's picture out and around as soon as he gets it. But he still can't spend a lot of time on this, right? I mean, given that he seems to be the only one who thinks it might actually be Talbot."

"Right."

Stephanie stood and went to the refrigerator. She brought a pitcher of iced tea back to the table, filled her glass, and then turned and looked Marian.

"So what we are going to do, my dear, is find him ourselves."

Marian put her fork down and studied Stephanie across the table. She watched as Stephanie drank from the glass and then smoked the cigarette for several seconds.

"You mean psychically."

"Yes."

Marian gazed into her plate and frowned. She knew Stephanie was waiting for her answer.

"You could, couldn't you?"

"I think so."

"Then when we find him, we call the police."

"Yes."

Marian stood and began removing dishes from the table. When Stephanie had finished the cigarette, she went to the sink and began filling it with hot water. She squeezed soap into the water and watched the suds foam up. It was only when she was putting the dishes into the sink that Marian spoke again.

"Tomorrow."

Stephanie looked at her. "Tomorrow. We'll start covering the city. If he's in Saint Augustine — and I believe he is — we'll find him. We'll start with the motels, and if that doesn't pay off, we'll cover every street."

Marian's eyes held Stephanie's for a minute. "It's dangerous."

"Well, we could make it worse, too." Stephanie frowned. "If he knows we're looking for him, he could make a move sooner than he might otherwise."

Marian stacked the leftover ham in a plastic container and snapped the lid shut. "Frankly," she said in a tight voice, "I would rather get it over with as quickly as possible anyway."

Stephanie nodded. "Then we start tomorrow."

1988

Wednesday
27
July

Marian watched her closely. Her eyes were closed, her head was bent slightly to one side, and the silver strands glinted in the dark hair where the sunlight touched it.

"He's not here, is he?"

Stephanie opened her eyes, propped her arm on the open car window, and stared at the small concrete-block motel beside the road. She shook her head and frowned. "I guess not."

They both sat still for several minutes. It was only eleven o'clock in the morning, and already the heat was wearing them down. The breeze that blew off the ocean beyond the dunes offered little relief.

Marian wiped perspiration from her forehead and upper lip. Her face felt gritty. "That's the last of the motels and hotels."

"Mmm."

"So maybe the bastard found an apartment — or he's living in a boarding house."

"Looks like it."

"Jesus H. Christ on a roller coaster. It could take half of forever to find him."

"You're becoming a mind reader." Stephanie started the VW and shifted into first gear but kept the clutch depressed. "Do you still want to do this?"

Marian shot her a wry smile. "The alternatives don't seem terribly attractive."

Stephanie held Marian's gaze for a minute, then pulled into the light traffic traveling north on Saint Augustine Beach. "No," she said, her mouth set in a grim line, "they don't. They don't at all."

Marian threw her bag onto the sofa and dropped down beside it, sighing heavily. "God, it's hot."

"Want some ice water?"

"With a vengeance. I'm going to plop into a cool bath. Why don't you come and talk to me."

Stephanie headed for the kitchen, poured two large glasses of water from the brown glass bottle they kept in the refrigerator, and returned to the bathroom. By the time she set one on the edge of the bathtub, the glasses were already dripping with condensation. Marian was sitting in the tub, adjusting the faucets so that lukewarm water splashed into the white porcelain. Stephanie closed the lid on the toilet and sat down, her elbows on her knees. She passed the ice-cold glass across her forehead.

Marian poured bubblebath into the tub and swirled the foam around with a washcloth, a frown on her face. "Well, where the hell could he be?"

"I don't know."

"We've covered the motels, the hotels, the apartment complexes. We've sat on every street. I think we've crawled over every damned scorching inch of Saint Augustine *and* the beaches."

Stephanie reached into her shirt pocket for a cigarette. "I don't know what else to do."

"But you still feel him, don't you? I mean, you still sense that he's somewhere near."

"Yes."

Marian washed her face and then splashed water from the flowing tap over her face. "Maybe it's someone like him. The same kind of — essence. The same kind of mental configuration or something."

"Maybe." Stephanie's voice was tired, resigned.

"But you don't think so."

"I don't know what to think anymore." She tapped ashes into the sink. "I don't know how to explain it, but there's something about him that's different. I mean, you could line up a dozen people who are *like* him, and there would still be a subtle difference with each one of them. The proverbial snowflake."

Marian turned off the faucet and held the washcloth up. "Wash my back?"

"Sure."

But Stephanie was now staring at the floor. Marian rolled her eyes upward and put the washcloth back into the water.

"They all *look* the same," Stephanie continued. "They all have six sides. All those things. But under a microscope, they are all distinctly different." She shook her head. "What I pick up is *him*. What I can't figure out is why I'm having such a hard time finding him. We go north one day, where the sensing is stronger, and it seems to dissipate when we get there. The next day, the sensing is stronger to the west, so we go west, and it just fades away again." She sighed heavily. "Maybe I'm leading us on a wild goose chase."

"No chance it's not him?"

There was a slight irritation in Stephanie's voice. "Of course there's a chance. You know that. I'm not a computer."

Marian lifted her eyebrows in mock astonishment. "No? Well, my goodness, I certainly thought you were."

Stephanie shot her a piercing look, then saw Marian's teasing smile and grinned. "Sorry. I guess I'm feeling guilty for putting you through this."

"I seem to recall making a choice on my own."

Stephanie laughed softly. "I do have a habit of forgetting things like that, don't I?"

"Mmm. Your protectiveness is endearing, sweetheart, but it does seem to create an awful lot of unnecessary guilt for you. You're lucky I'm not the kind of person who preys on that. I'd do you in pretty quickly."

"Why do you think I picked you?"

Marian took a drink of water from the glass on the edge of the tub and looked at Stephanie appraisingly. "Well," she finally replied, her face expressionless, "right now I'd say that if the direction of your gaze is any indication, your picking me had a lot more to do with my breasts than my sense of honor."

Stephanie stared at her, startled, then burst into loud laughter. Marian grinned and lost her own composure. As they laughed, the tension of the past week seemed to melt around them.

When their laughter finally subsided, Marian wiped tears from her eyes with the back of her hand. She took a deep breath and reached over to tap Stephanie's knee. "Okay. Enough levity, friend. Back to the problem at hand. Maybe he's gone. Could you be picking up his vibrations where he's been?"

Stephanie was still grinning. "I suppose. Anyway, we're not getting anywhere like this."

"Well, we could give it one more try. Then you've got to get back to work. Your clients are beginning to think you've deserted them. I've got almost another month before I go back to the grind, but you don't, my dear. Moneywise, we could make it quite easily, but pretty soon, they'll wonder if you've left town. By the way, I forgot to tell you — somebody by the name of Howard Claxton called this morning before you woke up. He wants you to call him later."

"Did he say what it was about?"

"Sort of. He seemed to be quite concerned that his mother is getting involved with a gold-digger or something. I was surprised that he was telling me his problems."

Stephanie smiled. "Howard doesn't particularly care about confidentiality. Actually, all he really needs is a friend to talk to. Practically anybody could tell him that the man his mother is interested in is hardly a gold-digger."

"Oh?"

"He's seventy-nine years old and owns two hotels in West Palm Beach. I don't care how much money Howard's mother has, her latest romance scarcely needs it. Howard is just concerned about his own part in her will."

"Any reason to be?"

Stephanie smiled. "None. Anyway, I'll give him a call after supper. Which reminds me, aren't you planning to meet Gary for lunch tomorrow?"

Marian looked down at the water for a moment and rubbed a non-existent spot on her knee. "Yes."

"What's the problem? I thought you enjoyed being with our detective friend."

"I do. And I'm interested in his knowledge of criminal psychology. Since I'm teaching that social-problems class this fall, I even thought he might have some references he could give me." She sighed. "But I'm afraid he's interested in a little more than friendship." She looked at Stephanie. "When he was over yesterday, while you were out with Karen and Bob, he made a pass at me. Nothing heavy, but it was obvious what he was getting at. I handled it very indirectly. I acted as if it hadn't happened, and that's just going to make it worse. To tell the truth, I don't understand why it happened at all."

"He finds you attractive."

Marian studied Stephanie for a moment. "You knew it already."

"It was pretty apparent."

"Not to me, it wasn't. Why didn't you say something?"

"I assumed if it ever came up, you would handle it."

"Yeah, I handled it, all right. I ignored it." She handed the washcloth to Stephanie again. "Are you ready *now* to wash my back?"

Stephanie looked at her curiously for a second, then comprehension dawned, and she smiled. "Sorry. I guess I was out in left field." She put the cigarette out in the ring of water in the sink drain and tossed it into the trashcan. She bent beside the tub and began rubbing Marian's back with long, slow strokes.

"Surely he knows we're lovers, Stef. He has to."

"How? We haven't told him, and we certainly don't hang all over each other when he's around. My dear, we aren't as transparent as you seem to think at times."

"Well, we haven't exactly kept our hands off each other, either. I mean, we do touch each other when he's around."

"So do other women who are friends. Besides, he's lonely. I

think when he and his wife separated, he really threw himself into his work. That's all he's had for a while. Then he becomes attracted to you, and he ignores anything he doesn't want to see."

Marian sighed. She leaned her head back and kissed Stephanie lightly. "My dear, I said my back. That is not my back. The purpose of this bath was to cool me off."

Stephanie grinned and pulled her hand back, but Marian caught it and held it on the inside of her thigh. "Well, I suppose I've got to talk to him about it." She released Stephanie's hand and picked up the glass of water.

"Yes, I suppose you do." Stephanie paused. "That is, if you want to."

Stephanie's voice had been deceptively light, and Marian set the glass down and looked up at her. "What's that supposed to mean? 'If I want to'?"

Stephanie shrugged. Marian was silent as she studied Stephanie's face, then she frowned. "What is this, Stef? What are you thinking?"

"I guess I feel a little threatened. He's attractive. He's a good person. The two of you obviously enjoy each other's company."

"You and he like each other, too."

"Yes. But you have a special communication with him. And I think he's still a little spooked by me."

Marian touched her cheek. "There's no reason for you to feel threatened. None at all."

Stephanie nodded and reached to pull the plug in the bathtub. "It's just that I don't blame him for wanting you."

Marian caught Stephanie's hand and held it against her stomach, the frown still on her face. Stephanie met her eyes.

"I don't want anyone but you," Marian said slowly. "It's important to me that you know that."

Stephanie nodded mutely. Her eyes were steady, but after several seconds, Marian saw a tear shining in the corner of her eye. Marian shook her head.

"Oh, Stef, I love you. I am *in* love with you. You must believe that by now. Are you still afraid I'll leave?" She searched Stephanie's face with concern.

Stephanie shook her head slightly. "No. I do believe you. But when I saw the two of you together the other day, it hit that place inside of me where the fear is." She sighed and looked away briefly. "It sounds foolish maybe — perhaps a little too romantic." She held Marian's eyes. "Don't laugh."

Marian smiled gently. "I make no promises. If it's funny, I might laugh." She touched Stephanie's cheek. "But I've got a feeling that what you're going to say I'm not going to find funny."

Stephanie looked away again, her voice was so soft it was almost a whisper. "Sometimes I think that when we met, I had retreated to this lonely cave inside myself. And you sat down outside the cave and held out your hand and waited very patiently. Little by little, I ventured out, and you touched me so very gently — with so much love — that I felt sometimes as if I might break apart from wanting you so much." She swallowed hard. "I still feel that way. And sometimes that little voice inside of me says, 'Be careful. It's dangerous to want someone that much.'" She smiled and looked at Marian again. "I guess I don't ever want to take you for granted."

Marian smiled, but her eyes were misty, too. She touched Stephanie's cheek again. "Take me for granted now," she whispered. "Go get a towel and dry me off, and we'll see if we can get rid of that little voice."

In the late-afternoon sun that filtered through the curtains in the bedroom, Marian propped herself on an elbow. "Stef, you know I don't want you to be here alone tomorrow."

"No. I thought we could go pick up the new carpet in the morning." She saw the grimace as Marian thought of Mr. Pye, and she touched the side of Marian's face. "Then, when we get back, I'll drop you off at The Half Shell to meet Gary. I want to go sit on the beach for a while and think about this. Gary can bring you to the beach when you're finished with lunch."

"Well —"

"I'll be okay. There'll be enough people out there that I definitely won't be alone."

"Okay. Just don't go anywhere else, all right? I know you can take care of yourself, and I don't like being a worrier, but I really would feel better about it."

"I know." Stephanie pulled Marian closer and caressed her

·107·

naked hip lightly. Marian buried her face in the side of Stephanie's neck.

"You know," Stephanie said, "after all this time, I still don't tell you enough that I love you."

Marian murmured something.

"Hmm?"

Marian lifted her head, and her eyes were soft in the dim light. "I said, you tell me every day. Even when you don't say it."

Stephanie caught Marian's face in her hands and pulled her down to kiss her once more.

1988

Saturday

30

July

1

Frank Talbot sat in the darkened room, his body slumped comfortably in the armchair facing the door that opened onto the porch. There was a new rug on the floor they had just put down this morning, and the sofa looked different somehow. New upholstery, maybe.

The blood must have ruined everything.

He was smiling. Occasionally, he chuckled under his breath.

The edge of the knife was razor-sharp. He ran his thumb carefully down the blade, reveling in its sharpness.

He looked at his watch. Twelve-fifteen.

He had been waiting a long time.

But it would be worth the wait. He was sure of it.

When he had planned the game, he didn't know about the other one — the younger one. She really suited his tastes more anyway. But the first time he saw her, he'd been puzzled. She was something new to contend with. He thought he'd have to work around her.

But then he had seen the bitch with her that night, sitting in the park facing the bridge. He had seen the way the bitch had touched her — and the way she had smiled back.

After that, he thought about them all the time.

They were together every night. The bitch touching her whore — touching a woman who should have been with a man.

He thought about it, let it fester in his gut until it boiled over into a renewed rage. Until he had more reasons to destroy the bitch than he would ever need.

To destroy both of them.

And the need to kill them had grown.

It was going to be even more beautiful than he could have ever imagined.

2

The Half Shell was not fancy in any sense of the word, but the food was plentiful, and the seafood was fresh and prepared well. There was a homey atmosphere about the wooden tables, the way customers joked with the waitresses — and, Marian considered wryly, its lack of romanticism. It was one of the main reasons she had suggested it. It was a great deal more suited to a friendly lunch than a romantic encounter.

"The shrimp were delicious. Thank you for treating me."

"You're quite welcome," Gary said, and he favored Marian with a rather lopsided smile that gave his normally rugged, tanned face a boyish quality that was classically disarming.

With his grin, Marian realized with a start what Stephanie must have seen before. In a sense, she had been quite accurate about Marian's attraction to the kind of man Gary was. But where Stephanie was off, Marian thought with a mental smile, was in the timing. Between that attraction and today were almost eight years and Stephanie herself.

Gary signaled across the lunch-hour hum and caught the waitress's eye. He held up the coffee cup, and she nodded back at him. When he put the cup down, he smiled at Marian again. "By the way, I'm surprised you're letting me buy you lunch. I thought feminists were supposed to be against anything except Dutch treat."

"Let's say we've mellowed in our old age," Marian said with a wry smile. "But I get to take you out next time. Assuming, of course, that your male ego doesn't get in the way."

"Where money is concerned, I have no ego," he grinned. Leaning forward, he put his elbows on the table. "Besides, if it means I get to have lunch again with such a beautiful woman, I would never refuse under any circumstances."

Marian glanced away for a moment. Then, deciding that bluntness was kinder than the evasion she had tried before, she met his eyes. "You know, Gary, I need to say something to you — get something clear with you."

"Oh?" His eyes became slightly guarded.

"Gary, I think you're building our relationship into something it's not."

"We're friends, right?" He shrugged his shoulders in an unconvincing gesture of nonchalance.

"Yes. We're friends. But I think you believe it could be something else. Perhaps something more. Gary, our relationship is friendship. It can never be anything else. I should have said it before now."

He leaned back in his chair and fiddled with the coffee cup for several seconds. When he spoke his voice was low, but there was an edge of intensity present. "I know it sounds like an old movie, but never is a long time."

Marian toyed briefly with her napkin and then looked at him again. "Gary, I love Stephanie. Do you understand that?"

"I know what your relationship is, if that's what you mean."

"No," she said quietly, "I don't think you do. If you did, you wouldn't have touched me the way you did the other day."

He was silent, and Marian stared at the napkin for a moment, thinking.

"Tell me. If I were married to a man — a friend of yours — would you have tried to kiss me when he wasn't there?"

Gary stared out the window toward San Marco Avenue and seemed to be studying the traffic intently. Finally he turned back, but he still avoided her eyes. "That's different."

Marian shook her head. "No, it's *not* different." She leaned forward to touch his hand, and he looked at it as if he were not sure he wanted to leave it there or pull it away.

"Gary, Stephanie is not just a good friend. And it's more than just a sexual thing we do. I know the male myth that presumes that it *is* just sexual, but I can assure you it's not true. Stephanie and I are lovers in every sense of the word."

He pulled his hand away and looked out the window. "I know that. But you're not married, are you?"

"No. We're not married." She felt a spark of anger, but it dissipated quickly. He was not being obstinate deliberately; he was protecting himself. "Not in the sense *you* mean married, because we don't have a piece of paper. But we do have a commitment to the relationship — to each other. And that commitment is based on trust and respect — and it includes sexual fidelity."

Gary shook his head as if he were trying to deny what she was saying. Then he put his arms on the table, leaned forward again, and stared into her eyes. "Marian, I *want* you. Not just sexually. I feel more for you than that."

"I know. And I'm flattered. But what you want is not going to happen."

Neither of them spoke for long minutes. Marian waited. Gary stared out the window.

His voice was soft when he finally spoke. "What if Stephanie were not there?"

"What do you mean?" She had felt a sudden prick of fear, and her tone was sharper than she had intended.

"I only meant, what if you didn't have a relationship with her?"

"You're talking about something that's not based in reality. I *do* have a relationship with her."

"But what if you didn't?"

Marian studied his face. He wanted, she knew, some hope that she couldn't give him. And if his friendship depended on that hope, then she would have to sacrifice the friendship. She sighed quietly. "Gary," she said as gently as she could, "it would be another woman."

He continued to stare out the window, and she did nothing to interrupt his thoughts. He was struggling with denial, with anger, with hurt, and he needed time to deal with all of them. She felt tenderness toward him, and she knew that if there had been any way she could have helped him with the struggle, she would have. But if he were to come through that struggle with his strength and dignity intact, he would have to do it for himself.

"I guess," he finally said, "it's going to take some time for me to understand." He looked back at her. "But I want you to know that I never wanted to treat your relationship lightly. Although I know I did by trying to ignore it." He brushed his hand through his sandy-brown hair and smiled almost sheepishly. "I guess what I'm saying is that I feel like an insensitive clod. I'm sorry."

Marian reached out and touched his hand again, and this time, he clasped hers warmly. "No, you're not an insensitive clod," she said. "Far from it. And I very much want you for a friend. Can you be that, Gary?"

He smiled again, and there was still pain in it, but he nodded. "Yes. I think I can. And Stephanie's, too, if she wants that."

"I'm sure she does."

He laughed softly then. "But I'm not going to promise that I won't feel the same way about you. I can only promise that I won't act on it."

Marian smiled. "I would say that's a very good start on a friendship."

In the car a few minutes later, Marian searched in her handbag for her swimsuit while Gary looked on, seemingly amused.

"Don't say it," she warned.

"Not me. At least I learned something from my marriage."

"Sexist pig," she countered. But finally, she groaned. "I forgot my swimsuit. Can you drop me off at the house?"

Gary frowned as he started the car. "I don't know if that's a good idea. How about if I wait for you?"

"Fine."

It took only a few minutes to cross downtown, but just as they pulled up in front of the house, a call came over the radio. When Gary ended the call, he said, "Look, I've got to get back right away. It'll just take you a minute, right?"

"Right. But why don't I drive down to the beach in my car? In fact, I think the suit is in the car anyway."

"Great. That would be very helpful."

Marian found the swimsuit in the back seat of the Buick and held it up with a smile. Gary waved back, made a turn at the cul-de-sac, and moved swiftly back up the street.

Marian, still smiling, slid under the steering wheel and plopped the bag on the seat beside her. But after a couple of minutes, it became apparent that the car keys were not there.

"Damn," she said softly, and she looked toward the house.

3

Stephanie sat up and toweled the perspiration off her face, throat, and upper chest. The sun broiled down white-hot, and she felt vaguely as if she were on a roasting spit that had come to a dead stop. A piece of sand gritted between her teeth.

The sea ran up on the beach and retreated; a small child several yards down the wide expanse of white sand laughed delightedly as his father piled up a sand castle into shape.

Stephanie closed her eyes, took a deep breath, and exhaled slowly. She breathed deeply, evenly for a few minutes. Finally, the sounds of the ocean and the other sunbathers became fuzzy and soft as she opened herself to the light trance state. For several minutes, as her external senses were stilled, she allowed a single question to fill her mind.

Where is he?

But all she could see was Marian standing on the front porch, pushing the key into the lock.

As Marian opened the door, the vision faded.

After a few minutes, Stephanie opened her eyes and squinted at the brightness of the beach.

Perhaps her concentration wasn't intense enough. The strain of the past few days had been draining.

4

When he heard a car on the gravel in front of the house, he arose and crept silently across the floor. He positioned himself behind the door, the knife poised.

The screen door squeaked open, and he held his breath, his eyes on the doorknob.

It did not turn.

The screen door squeaked again, and he heard footsteps walking back along the driveway. He let his breath out, drew aside the curtain a couple of inches, and peered out cautiously.

It was the bitch's woman. She was opening the car door and

pulling out a beach bag. She walked back toward the house, her hand in the bag. Halfway to the door, she pulled out a key.

He wiped a hand across his mouth. And then he smiled. Good-looking hips. Nice ass. Something a man could hold onto. And then the dizzying rage slammed into his gut again.

A man! he screamed inside. *Not some filthy lezzie queer. A man!*

He stared at her full breasts, soft under the blouse. They moved gently, swayed freely with every step she took. Her hair looked silky. He wanted to touch it. He felt himself growing hard. "Just a few more minutes, boy," he whispered to himself. "Just a few more minutes."

He grinned as he slid behind the door once more and saw the doorknob jiggle as the key was inserted.

5

Stephanie rolled over on the beach towel and rested her head on her arms. She was just tired. All she needed was a short nap. But she kept musing on the vision. Marian unlocking the door. Strange. *Marian unlocking the door.*

Suddenly, she shivered violently as a sliver of fear clawed its way up her spine and chilled the back of her neck.

No. Marian was with Gary. They would meet her here.

But a hideous chant began thundering in her head, pounding at her temples.

Kill the bitch. Kill the bitch. Kill the bitch.

She whipped over, bolted upright, and stared vacantly at the waves that flowed in, curved along the sand, foamed, flowed out again.

But then she knew it was true.

She had seen Marian because he was with her.

He was with Marian.

Her senses screaming, she bolted to her feet, grabbed up her jeans with her wallet and keys, and shoved her feet into the leather sandals. The remainder of the things she had brought with her were left behind as she ran for the wooden stairs leading up over the dune.

Sand boiled up from under her feet; she felt as if she were running in slow motion, her calves aching after only several steps in the deep sand, as if she were running in quicksand.

Reaching the steps, she pulled herself up them with her free hand as much as with her feet. At the top, she dashed across the rough concrete floor of a shelter where a family was spreading out a picnic lunch. She banged into a large cooler, stumbled, and pitched forward onto the concrete. A stab of pain shot through her knee and her palms as she fell. A woman gasped, and a man began getting up from the table to help her, but she had already scrambled to her feet and was running again by the time he reached her.

She breathed heavily, more from the terror than from the running. She could feel her face distorted with fear as she barreled down the stairs to the parking lot. She stumbled as her foot missed a step near the bottom, but she caught herself on the railing, righted herself, and ran on.

A telephone. Telephone. She should call the police. From where she was on Anastasia Island, she was closer to the Saint Augustine Beach police, but that would do her no good. They wouldn't send a car to Saint Augustine. She was only seven or eight minutes from home if she really floored it, but the Saint Augustine police could get somebody there faster than she could make it.

Reaching the car, she stared up and down the shrub-lined pebble-and-concrete road. Sweat dripped into her eyes and burned. She wiped the jeans across her face.

The telephone by the restrooms.

She turned and ran for the concrete-block building in back of the parking lot. When she reached it, she yanked the receiver off the hook. It was useless; the cord running from the receiver to the telephone was disconnected and dangled loosely. With a groan, she flung it into the sand and ran back to the car.

There was a gas station where the road from the park entered A-1-A.

She yanked at the car door. Locked. She searched in the jeans for the keys, but when she found them, they fell to the ground. Hands shaking, she retrieved the ring, found the key again, and unlocked the door. Jerking the door open, she threw herself under the steering wheel and gunned the motor to life. She backed out with a screech, shoved the car into gear, and squealed out of the parking lot onto the road.

Scrub palmettos and live oaks flew by as she pushed at the accelerator. But she felt as if she were on a treadmill. The short distance to the highway crawled by.

When she reached the gas station, she screeched to a halt in front of the door. She jumped out and flung herself through the doorway.

An older man leaned back in a chair, his feet propped up on the metal desk. He looked up as she slammed into the desk, breathing hard.

"Yes? Can I help you?" He almost fell backwards in the chair as he tried to get up quickly.

"Telephone," she whispered hoarsely.

"What, Miss?"

She slammed her fist on the desk and tried to calm her breathing. "A telephone. *Do you have a telephone in here?*"

He shook his head and stepped back from her. "No. Sorry. The only one's in the garage," he pointed, "and it's broke."

"That's impossible," Stephanie rasped. She dropped her head and hit the desk with her fist again. He backed away a few more steps.

If she stopped again, she thought, it would only slow her down. It would take time to explain to the police. And it would take time for them to dispatch a car. And it would take time for them to get there.

Time. It was something she didn't have.

She whirled and shot through the door, leaving the man with a startled expression on his face.

She squealed the car onto the highway once more, barely slowing to check for traffic. She shook the steering wheel with clenched fists.

Perhaps he wasn't with her yet. Perhaps she had just sensed he was going to be.

Her body was tight with fear, and she pushed the car's speed up to seventy. Eighty. The VW screamed at her.

She tried to reassure herself. It did not *have* to happen. Events could be set in motion, but they could be interrupted.

They could be changed.

She clung to this thought now with every ounce of her strength, trying desperately to force out the thought that she would be too late.

She sat stiffly at the wheel. "Please, God," she whispered. *"Please."*

She instinctively started to slow for a yellow light at an intersection and then jabbed at the accelerator. She shot through a red light, narrowly missing a motorcyclist who had edged into the intersection a second sooner. She watched the rearview mirror, saw the motorcycle righted, and swallowed hard.

She weaved in and out of the traffic heading toward Saint Augustine, juggling the brake and gas pedal, leaving angry drivers in her wake.

Finally, she was in sight of the Bridge of Lions, and her breathing slowed a little. She was close now. Only a couple of minutes maybe.

But as the wheels of the VW gained the upward slope of the bridge, it became apparent that there was another problem. Traffic moving across the span was moving much more slowly than usual, and she caught up with it in seconds. There must be a slowdown on the other side. She almost sobbed with frustration and fear. She pounded her fist on the dashboard.

But just as the traffic seemed to be flowing more quickly, the impossible happened.

The second car in front of her stopped as the light on the bridge flashed yellow. She braked hard. Cars began piling up behind her. The light turned red. And then the crossing arm that had pointed upwards to her right now jerked once and swung down over the bridge, halting traffic in her lane.

Her knuckles whitened. *No, God, no!*

As she watched in horrified silence, the bridge began to open. Began to yawn into the sky as though it might swallow the clouds that scutted across the bay. And in the water of the Matanzas River to the left, a pleasure boat with a tall mast that stabbed at the sky sailed toward that opening.

A soft scream caught in her throat, and she clenched her fists and smacked them on the steering wheel. She looked around frantically. There was no room to turn on the bridge. She was locked in. She had stopped just inches from the bumper of the car in front of her, and the car behind her had done the same. And there would have been no room anyway to move the VW out of its position in line.

And if she had been able to get off the bridge, she knew, it would take more time now to get to a phone than if she waited.

So she sat imprisoned in the car, sweat streaming down her face, sweat soaking her body, small cries of agony escaping her lips.

It was several minutes before the wait was over, and by the time the bridge started closing, she was in the grip of a terror that threatened to overwhelm her with its intensity.

As the bridge locked into place once more, she looked down to her right and saw a suntanned couple with linked arms laughing and waving up to the cars on the bridge.

The traffic began to crawl again.

Move, she screamed silently. *Move!*

Finally, as she reached the end of the bridge, she screeched off and swerved around a car whose driver had slowed to study street signs. She tore through the red light and onto Avenida Menendez, the continuation of San Marco Avenue as it curved through downtown. She barely missed a camper that came at her from the opposite direction, and unexpectedly, she was assaulted anew by a sense of hideous evil. She gasped harshly and struggled to keep the car under control as she careened toward the Dolls in Wonderland building on the right, ignoring angry horn blasts and squealing tires. She was shaking violently.

The blocks seemed to inch by, although she had pushed her speed up as far as she dared to avoid going off the road as she rounded corners.

Six blocks from the house, children playing in a yard let a ball slip out of their hands. It rolled toward the street, and a small boy in a striped t-shirt ran after it, laughing delightedly.

She stabbed at the brakes and swerved wildly; the back of the car went into a sickening slide.

The child, his face a mask of sudden fright, stumbled back from the sidewalk and sat down hard, his face screwing up, readying itself for tears.

The shaking increased until she was barely able to hold the wheel. She passed her hand across her eyes and swallowed, but her mouth was dry.

A block away, she saw Gary's car in front of the house. He was just standing up. A uniformed police officer was getting out on the other side. She screeched to a halt, and the tires failed to grab at the sand and slid several feet. She jumped out of the car and ran toward the house.

"Stephanie," Gary yelled, "what's wrong?"

"*Marian,*" she shouted hoarsely. "*He's with Marian!*"

Gary caught up with her just as she pounded up the steps. She slammed into the screen door with one hand, jerked it open, crossed the porch, and pulled frantically at the inside door.

It was locked.

Gary's face was hard as he opened his jacket and pulled out his gun. He waved the other police officer around to the back of the house.

"Marian!" she shouted at the door while she stabbed at the key-hole with a shaking hand and missed the lock.

She pounded on the door with her free hand and shouted again.

Finally Gary took the key from her and motioned her to move back from the door. He inserted the key in the lock, and she noticed his hand was trembling slightly as well. He turned the key and, with one abrupt movement, opened the door and slammed it back against the inside wall. It hit hard and swung back, coming to a rest half-closed.

Stephanie started to rush forward, but he grabbed her arm.

"He's not here," Stephanie said. "He's gone."

He looked at her for a few seconds and then nodded. Pushing gently at the door, he peered into the room, black in contrast to the brightness outside. With a sigh, he looked back toward the street.

Stephanie pushed past him and stared into the gloom, her heart pounding against her ribs, her palms wet with fear.

A half-sob escaped her lips.

He had been there. A lamp had fallen onto the floor in the corner, the coffee table had been pushed out of place. Everything that had been on the table — books, magazines, a cup half-filled with tea this morning — was strewn about the room.

Stephanie jogged through the house to the hall and the bedroom at the end. She stopped herself as she reached the door.

Everything she had feared was facing her.

Marian lay spread-eagled on the bed, face down, her head turned toward the opposite wall. Her arms and legs were tied with lengths of white clothesline that ran to the bedframe.

She was gagged — and nude.

Stephanie approached the bed, terror constricting her breathing. "Marian?" she whispered.

As her eyes grew accustomed to the dim light, she saw the ugly, dark bruises scattered across Marian's back, her hips, the insides of her thighs. The stink of fear and sweat was heavy in the room.

Gary stood in the doorway now, his face averted.

As Stephanie drew near the bed, Marian's head moved haltingly on the pillow. Stephanie whispered her name again.

Slowly, Marian's face turned toward Stephanie. A thin line of blood had seeped through the swath of white cloth across her mouth and trickled down her chin. Perspiration dotted her forehead; her hair fell damply across her face.

"I'll get an ambulance," Gary said hoarsely and turned away.

As Stephanie fumbled with the gag, she murmured reassuringly, over and over, "It's okay, honey, I'm here. It's okay, I'm here."

Marian's eyes fluttered open and settled on Stephanie's face. They were glassy, vacant.

Stephanie released the gag carefully, but the cloth stuck to the tear at the corner of the bruised mouth, and the wound began bleeding again.

The pain flooded into Stephanie's chest and stomach. It rushed at her, threatened to split her apart, and she gasped as she opened herself to it as fully as she could in order to know what to do next.

As she worked with stiff fingers at the ties around Marian's wrists, the deep green-blue eyes opened again. Through dry lips, Marian murmured, "Stef?" Stephanie touched Marian's forehead gently and pushed back the damp hair, and Marian's eyes closed again.

As Stephanie fumbled with the bonds around Marian's ankles, the extent and brutality of the assault became even more painfully apparent. Minute tears of flesh had bled and spotted the sheet beneath Marian's body, and the sheet she lay on was damp, an acrid odor of urine strong in the air.

When she finished, Stephanie grabbed at the terrycloth bathrobe that hung across the chair, draped it over Marian's still form, and sat gently on the bed. She touched Marian's arm and whispered her name.

The eyes fluttered open again and filled with tears.

"You're here," she breathed, her voice barely audible in the darkened room.

"Yes." Stephanie touched her cheek and stood, intending to find a washcloth, but Marian clutched at her hand. Her eyes were wide with fear.

"Don't leave me — please don't leave me. . ."

Stephanie shook her head. "No." She bent down and gently kissed the corner of the torn mouth. Marian's breath was pungent, salty, and Stephanie realized with a jolt that the invasion of her body had been complete.

A sob rose in Stephanie's throat, and she closed her eyes tightly and tried to hold back the tears. But they came anyway, and she soon gave up the effort and allowed them to stream down her face as she smoothed her hand over Marian's forehead and whispered tenderly to her.

Gary came back to the doorway. The ambulance would be there within minutes, and he had planned to tell Stephanie. But he stopped at the door.

As he watched the two women on the bed, saw the tenderness and pain in Stephanie's eyes as she held Marian and rocked her with such gentleness, saw the trust and love in Marian's eyes, he felt an ache in his chest that he knew would be there for a long time. At that moment, he was aware that there was nothing more he wanted than to be the one holding Marian.

And at the same time, he understood quite clearly that Marian had told him the truth. She would never be able to give him what he wanted from her.

6

"I convinced her to let me give her something for the pain. She wouldn't take anything to help her sleep. I told her she could talk to you later, but she's a stubborn woman."

Dr. Karen Fowler tore a sheet off the prescription pad and handed it to Stephanie. "That's for the pain. She'll need it for another day or two."

She motioned Stephanie to a chair near the nurse's station in the hall and sat down next to her. "Look, Stephanie, you know Marian will heal herself — she's strong. But I *am* concerned about her. If it had been a simple rape —"

Stephanie flinched. "Simple? What in God's name is a *simple* rape, Karen?"

Karen rubbed her eyes in a gesture of weariness. "Sorry. Poor choice of words. What I mean is, if her attacker had cornered her, raped her, and then ran, it would be a little different. It's a terrifying, humiliating experience under any circumstances. But this kind of sadistic cruelty — the brutality — some of the shock she went into for a while had to do with the physical trauma. But not all of it." She frowned. "You heard her when she told the police what happened. It sounded as if she were talking about someone else. It's down there eating at her."

The two women leaned back in the chairs and were silent for a few minutes. Finally, Karen turned her head toward Stephanie again.

"And you, my friend. How are you?"

"Angry. Scared."

"And hurting?"

Stephanie avoided Karen's searching gaze for a minute and then met her eyes. "Yes. Hurting."

"You can't blame yourself," Karen murmured.

Stephanie smiled wryly. "You sound like Marian."

"She's an incredibly intelligent woman," Karen replied, and her mouth twitched a bit at the corner in a small smile. She stood and shoved her hands into the pockets of her white jacket. "Look, Stephanie, why don't you see her and then go over to our house. Bob's there, and I'll be along shortly. Get a good night's sleep. Pick up Marian in the morning."

Stephanie shook her head. "Thanks, Karen. I think I'll stay. I'll wash up a little in the restroom. There'll be plenty of time to sleep later."

Karen nodded. "Well, just remember to take care of yourself, too. Okay?"

"Sure. Thanks."

Stephanie watched as Karen walked down the hall and disappeared around the corner before she got up and went to Marian's room.

"Don't clean up before I get home."

"Why? Are you sure?"

"Yes. I have to be able to see it, feel it again. I don't want to even think about it, but I have to. If I get home and it looks like it never happened, I'll just push it further away from me. I can't do that."

Marian reached a hand from under the sheet and touched Stephanie's knee. "Promise me. I know you want to push it away, and so do I, but it's important not to."

Stephanie leaned forward in the chair, then took Marian's hand and held it between her own hands without speaking. The color had come back into Marian's face, but there were dark circles under her eyes, as if she had not slept for a long time. Her words were still low; her voice sounded slightly hoarse.

Stephanie sighed. There was wisdom in what Marian said. Walking back into her home as it had been before the attack would be putting the evidence of her pain and humiliation away where it could fester for years. It would be best for Marian to confront that reality, no matter how traumatic it might be.

And the other was true, too. Stephanie's natural impulse was to push it away, to close the wound as quickly as possible, regardless of what she knew was best.

She nodded. "You're right. As usual."

Marian smiled a little. "Don't be afraid, sweetheart. I'm going to be okay. Really." She squeezed Stephanie's hand. "But what about you?"

"Karen just asked me that." She sighed again. "You know, so many people seem to think that I'm the strong one. My clients, our acquaintances, strangers we meet, even some of our friends. Just because I don't show how I feel. But you're really the stronger one, you know. You always have been."

"You *are* strong. You are."

"Maybe a little. But not like you." She arose from the chair beside the bed, leaned over, and kissed Marian gently on the forehead. Her voice was soft, intense. "But I promise you, this time you *can* lean. As much as you need to, for as long as —"

Marian put her fingers across Stephanie's lips. "Shh. No more. You've always been there for me. Always." She smiled. "Why do you think I'm so much in love with you?"

"I'm going to cry."

"Good. You probably need to. I know you're holding back a lot, too. Lie down with me and cry and hold me." She turned slowly onto her side, and although she made no sound, Stephanie saw the pain in her eyes.

"I don't think there's room. I might hurt you."

"We'll make room. I need you. I can stand the physical pain right now more than I can stand being away from you."

So, with infinite care and tenderness, Stephanie lay on the small bed and cradled Marian in her arms until the slivers of light that peered into the shade-darkened room sighed and slipped away into the night.

7

It was pitch-black, but he couldn't risk turning on a light. He closed the kitchen door behind him and dug into his pocket for matches. Lighting one, he looked around in the gloom, got his bearings, then blew out the match. He spat on his rubber-gloved fingers and tapped at the match-head to cool it, then slipped it back into his pocket.

He moved to the refrigerator and opened the door. He could see well enough with the light, but it was just dim enough so that it would not be seen from the yard with the curtains closed. Besides, there were no houses back there — just scrubby woods past the yard and then the water down past the hill.

He studied the contents of the refrigerator for a few seconds before he saw what he might be able to use — a brown glass quart bottle. He opened the top and peered in. No smell. He tipped it and touched his tongue to the rim. Water.

He smiled a little in the dim glow of the light.

Reaching into a pocket, he drew out a small jar. He unscrewed the cap and tapped the bottom of the jar. The contents of the jar splashed into the water with a satisfying plop.

He grinned.

A noise from the front startled him. Shutting the refrigerator door, he reached for the kitchen door behind him and opened it. Lights flooded through the small windowpanes in the front door and flashed aross the kitchen floor.

The hair stood up on the back of his neck as he heard the car door slam and footsteps on the driveway.

He pulled the knife out and snapped it open, then plastered himself against the wall just inside the door and listened. Seconds ticked by in silence.

He jerked his head toward the back door. Maybe they were coming around the house. Quickly he crossed the kitchen and stood in the corner behind the outside door so he could not be seen when it was opened.

But nothing happened.

After several minutes, he ducked across the kitchen again, slid around the doorjamb, and crouched near the floor.

Still nothing.

Then a squeak.

He was breathing rapidly now, and his palms were sweating inside the gloves.

When nothing else happened, he lay on his belly and pulled himself across the floor, the knife held tightly, until he was just under the window to the left of the living room door. Raising his body slowly, he lifted an edge of the curtain and peered out.

A man sat hunched on the swing, bent over, his head resting in his hands.

Talbot frowned. He stood up quietly, crossed to the door, and looked out the small-paned window at the top.

A cop car. *A goddamned cop car.* He felt the fear poke at his stomach again. *Was he going to get to the back door and find himself cornered?* His breathing sounded loud. Too loud.

He crossed to the window again and looked out. He stared at the figure on the swing.

As he watched, the man reached inside his jacket and pulled out a notepad and pencil. After writing for a minute, he got up from the swing and left the porch, where he turned and stuck a piece of paper on the hook of the mailbox. Then he walked back down the driveway and got into the patrol car. The headlights stabbed at the house again, and Talbot ducked as they shot through the windows in the door.

He waited a couple of minutes, put the knife away, then opened the door and made his way cautiously across the porch. Opening the screen door, he pulled the paper off the hook.

Back inside the house, he lit another match and opened the folded piece of paper. A grin crept across his face.

So the stupid bastard was sorry, was he? Well, they were all going to be a fucking lot sorrier before he was finished with them.

He balled up the note and started to shove it into his pocket, but a new thought occured to him — a pleasing thought.

In the bedroom, he lit another match and looked around with satisfaction at the dissarray. There was a stale smell in the room. The whore had pissed all over the bed. She had been scared the whole time. Just like the gook in Nam. From the minute he had put the knife to her throat.

And she had fought him most of the time. Until he had tied her down. She had been quiet then for a while. But his fists had changed that.

Then how she had screamed — even muffled, he could tell they were long, hard screams. Nice screams. Until she couldn't scream anymore.

Not even when he'd treated her the way she deserved to be treated.

She had thought he was going to kill her. That kind of fear had been in her eyes.

He had thought about blindfolding her, but there was really no need to do that. They already knew who he was. What he looked like.

Or they thought they did.

He grinned in the darkness and wiped his hand across his mouth.

He'd even thought about cutting her eyes out, like he had the cat's. Just slip the knife into the corner and pop them right out. That would have been a nice touch.

But there would be time for that later.

First, they were going to see each other suffer. For as long as he wanted them to. He had learned ways to do that in Nam.

The bitch was going to watch her whore die.

Then the bitch would die.

He tossed the note onto the bed and laughed.

He was still grinning when he left by the back door, disappeared into the tangled live oaks, and headed down the hill toward the inlet.

1988

Sunday
31
July

1

Down the hall from Marian's hospital room, Stephanie splashed cold water on her face from the tap in the restroom and patted it off with a stiff paper towel from the dispenser. Reaching into the back pocket of the slacks Karen had loaned her, she fished a comb out and pulled it through her hair while her reflection in the mirror stared back solemnly. Her eyes felt grainy and heavy from sleeplessness. She pocketed the comb and leaned stiff-armed on the chilly white porcelain at the edge of the row of sinks.

He was playing with them.

Playing.

Her frustration and anger mounted as she turned that knowledge over in her mind, and she curled her hands into fists and dug her nails into her palms until it grew too painful.

He could have killed Marian, but he hadn't.

The next time, he would.

She lowered her head and sighed heavily. Why hadn't she been able to find him?

Why?

It was as if the roots of a dead tree submerged in a dark lake had caught a priceless treasure in their grasp and were holding it just out of her reach. No matter how often she dove into the lake, she couldn't pry the treasure from the roots that entrapped it.

The answer was there, she knew, if only she could find a way to release it.

She stood there for long minutes, then shook her head in wearied resignation. She was tired, too exhausted to face the darkness and coldness of that lake right now.

And in that moment of letting go, the tangled roots seemed to sigh in resignation with her. The treasure popped loose from its prison, shivered its way through the darkness, and bobbed to the surface amidst brilliant shafts of light that sparkled over the water.

The answer flashed across her mind with such suddenness, such crystal-like clarity, that she gasped slightly.

It was so simple, really.

She raised her head and stared into the mirror again. Her eyes stared back at her in surprise.

It was so simple, it was almost perfect.

2

"Are you okay?"

"Compared to what?" Marian was ashen-faced, her mouth set in a grim line of control as she stood in the doorway of the bedroom.

"Sorry. It was a stupid question."

Marian's eyes flitted briefly to Stephanie's. "You look like you're walking on eggshells."

"I suppose." Stephanie rubbed her forehead wearily. "Look, why don't you get clean sheets. I'll take the mattress pad off, and we'll have everything cleaned up in no time."

"Okay." But Marian did not move. "What's that?"

Stephanie followed her gaze.

Marian walked toward the bed, flinching slightly on the first step. She picked up the piece of paper and unfolded it.

"What is it?"

"A note from Gary," Marian said. Her eyebrows pulled into a frown.

"Gary?" Stephanie frowned as well, then she closed her eyes as realization dawned.

"My God," Marian whispered. "My God, he's been here." Her eyes widened with fear, and she flung the paper back onto the bed. Her body began trembling, and she rubbed her hands up and down her bare arms as if she were chilled, although it was a hot, muggy morning and they had been perspiring earlier. She put her hands to her mouth, but she only succeeded in muffling the words. *"He was here again!"*

Stephanie took Marian's hands and held them tightly for a moment, then she put her arms around her. "It's okay. He's not here now," she said quietly. In vain, she tried to hold Marian's eyes with her own. Finally, she took Marian's face in her hands and held it still. "Marian," she said firmly, "you're running away. Come back."

Marian stared at her, unseeing, for several seconds, then she closed her eyes briefly. When she opened them again, the glassiness was gone. She took a deep breath and let it out slowly. Tears pooled on her bottom lashes and spilled down her cheeks. She pressed her face against Stephanie's shoulder, her body relaxing slightly, and Stephanie held her closely.

"What was he doing here, Stef?"

"Probably just letting us know he *was* here."

Marian closed her eyes again. "Bastard," she whispered. "Goddamned bastard."

Stephanie stood in the middle of the living room and waited for Marian to get a glass of water. She was wondering where to start on the disorder around her when she heard the horrified scream and the sound of shattering glass. She whirled and ran for the kitchen.

Marian was standing by the sink, her body trembling violently. In the pool of water and broken brown glass at her feet swam the dead, glassy, staring eyes of Mr. Pye.

Stephanie looked away and fought for control over her own emotions, then she swallowed hard and forced her legs to move. She grasped Marian's arm firmly to pull her away, but Marian resisted strongly. With sharp fierceness, she shook off Stephanie's hand, her face distorted with a rage Stephanie had never seen there before.

Stephanie forced herself to remain where she was standing, rooted herself to the floor, would not allow herself to back away, but Marian's anger slammed into her body like a wave, pounded at her head, and she felt suddenly, unbearably nauseated. She swayed backwards and leaned against the table for support. The watery eyes stared up at her.

Marian was enclosed in her own world of pain, though, and was completely oblivious to Stephanie's reaction. She turned and slammed her fists on the counter, and her screams of rage and frustration filled the house. She allowed the storm of anger and pain to engulf her, to sweep through her completely. She did not try to still it, did not try to hold it back or control it. She simply allowed it to take her where it would.

Finally, after long minutes, the storm broke its main force into smaller currents and eddies, and she slammed her hands down once more and was quiet for several seconds. It was only then, in the aftermath of the larger storm, that she doubled over, her arms hugging herself, and allowed the huge, wracking sobs to shake her body.

Stephanie took a deep breath and pushed herself away from the table. She pulled a chair out and eased Marian into it, then she knelt and held her hands outstretched on Marian's knees. Marian grasped and squeezed them hard, until Stephanie flinched slightly from the pressure.

When the sobs lessened, Marian gazed at Stephanie through the tears that continued to stream down her face. She seemed to notice only then that their hands were intertwined tightly, and she loosened her grip. Her breath came in gasps for a few seconds longer and then calmed. Stephanie searched Marian's eyes, and Marian nodded her head slightly and caressed Stephanie's hands. Finally, she leaned forward and hugged Stephanie closely. Her cheek was wet against Stephanie's.

Stephanie returned the warm embrace and felt her body relax with relief. Marian had begun the healing process that would lead her back to wholeness.

But her own eyes, Stephanie considered, seemed strangely dry.

"Marian?"

"Hmm?"

The porch swing squeaked in the darkness, and a breeze wafted the warm, heavy-sweet fragrance of gardenia to them from the yard.

"I want you to leave."

"Leave?"

"Until it's over."

"No."

"I think it would be best if—"

"No. I'm not leaving you."

"But I think he's coming back, and—"

"Correction, lady. You *know* he's coming back."

There was a long silence.

"Yes."

"Sorry, Stef, but the bastard's going to have to deal with both of us. I am *not* leaving you."

For a long time, there was only the squeak of the swing and the rustle of the palms in the soft night.

"Stef?"

"Yes."

"When?"

"I don't know. A while yet. It's part of the game for him. So we become even more afraid."

The porch swing squeaked again, and the scent of gardenia seemed to grow heavier, sweeter, in the warm darkness.

"Stef?"

"Yes."

"It's working. I'm more afraid."

There was silence, and then a tired sigh.

"I know."

And almost as if Stephanie were tacking it on as an afterthought, she added, "Me, too."

1988

1

Marian took off her reading glasses and lay them on top of the scatter of papers on the coffee table. She leaned back on the sofa and rubbed her eyes.

Stephanie pushed herself away from the doorjamb and smiled. "Finished?"

"Almost. I've got the course outline done, anyway. All I have to do now is get my notes into some recognizable order."

"Well, you've got time."

"Mmm. Speaking of time, did Gary say when he'd be over?"

"Six or so. I thought I'd make the salad now. We can do the pasta after he gets here."

"Sounds good. The sauce should be ready any time we are."

Stephanie left the living room, and Marian put her glasses back on, but after a few minutes of shuffling through the papers, she took them off again and frowned. She looked toward the kitchen, where she heard Stephanie opening the refrigerator door.

Something was bothering Stephanie that she wasn't saying, Marian mused. She had asked about it earlier, but Stephanie's reply had been evasive, and when questioned about the evasiveness, she had closed herself off even further. Marian was used to the preoccupation that occurred periodically, but this time it was different somehow. Stephanie was not just wrapped up in her thoughts — she seemed to be hiding them deliberately.

Marian began gathering up the papers. There was really no point in working any longer right now. She was having a hard time concentrating.

The tension, of course, was affecting them both, she considered. Not knowing when the next attack might come — not knowing what it would be — from where it would come. But they had installed one of the best alarm systems available, Gary had a patrol car cruising by at least every hour during the day and more frequently at night, and he was spending most of his off-duty hours with them. So was it really protection that Stephanie was worried about? And if not that, then what?

Marian rubbed her eyes again and sighed softly. It was useless to dwell on it. There were times when she could probe at Stephanie. Something like running your hands over a wall where you knew a hidden panel existed, and then you'd touch the right spot and the panel would swing open, revealing what was behind it. And sometimes she felt she could probe for days and not find the right spot. In the beginning of their relationship, she had done a lot more probing a lot more often, but she found herself doing less of it as the years passed. Now, she seemed to intuit when it could be pursued successfully and when it couldn't. Also, she had to admit with a small inward smile at herself, as the years passed, she had learned that when Stephanie erected that wall between them, it didn't mean her love had changed. In the beginning, Marian had not always been sure of that.

Now, she knew, was not a time for probing — it would get her nowhere. When Stephanie was ready to tell her what was happening, she would tell her.

2

Martin Leiberman patted his inside coat pocket and felt the bulge there. It had been a good day. In fact, the day's proceeds would mean a hefty deposit tonight indeed. A very good day. Then on home to Sarah's fine meat loaf.

He took his hat off the rack behind him and settled it on his white hair, then buttoned the sweater his wife had knitted him for his sixty-first birthday, just two years before. He unlocked the swing-up door in the counter and caught sight of the fading pawn-shop sign in the front window. He made a mental note again to call the painter in the morning.

As he started to open the door, he reached into the display window and readjusted the hunting and sporting goods he had taken in during the day. They were almost new, purchased from a woman whose husband had died recently. And he had given her a good price for them, too, he thought. A little more, actually, than maybe he should have. But she had reminded him of Sarah, and he had felt sympathy for the lady. Anyway, he would still make a good profit, and the goods would go quickly.

He opened the front door and glanced up and down the street. A young couple out for a walk in the late evening passed him. It wasn't quite dark yet. In the winter, when the sun was down as he got ready to leave, he sometimes called one of the nice young police officers who patrolled the area, and they always seemed happy to escort an anxious old man to the bank.

"Bah," he snorted. "No reason for that tonight."

Martin Lieberman turned and locked the door to the shop, touched his pocket again, and set off down the street, whistling under his breath. But as he walked past the alley between the shop and the automotive-parts store next door, a hand gripped his arm and pulled him into the alley. His startled cry was cut off sharply, and he felt his head explode with lights. A well of blackness sucked at him and drew him into it.

Fifteen minutes after his wife Sarah had called them, the Saint Petersburg police found him lying unconscious behind the garbage cans in the alley. When he regained consciousness, he was unable to describe his assailant. He had seen nothing.

1988

1

Stephanie leaned over to give Marian a brief kiss, then straightened and patted Marian's arm on the car window.

"Take care of yourself. Say hello to your mother for me. I'm sorry I won't get to see her this time."

"I will." Marian smiled. "You know, she's really disappointed you're going to Tallahassee instead of coming to see her. I think she believes you're her other daughter."

Stephanie grinned. "Tell her we'll get down again soon. Fort Lauderdale's not the other side of the world."

Stephanie started to move away, but Marian caught her hand and squeezed it gently. "I'll call you tonight."

"Well, maybe I'd better call you. I'm not sure I'll be staying with the Campbells. They're setting up the readings in their home, but I might stay with Julie and go on to Tallahassee in the morning."

Marian arched an eyebrow. "Okay. Just be sure you remember that she's an *old* lover, dear. You've got enough to keep you busy right here."

"She said, as if she needed to worry," Stephanie smiled wryly.

She crossed to the other side of Gary's car, where Gary stuck his hand out the window. She took it, then on impulse, she planted a kiss on his cheek. His face broke into the boyish grin.

"Are you sure you trust me with her?" he asked, and Stephanie laughed. If he could joke about it, the three of them were well on their way to becoming friends. She leaned over, stared at Marian, then gave him a mock-solemn look.

"I'm not sure. Maybe you'd better lock yourself in your room tonight if you don't want her to bother you."

Gary guffawed, and Stephanie caught Marian's wink before she smiled and stepped back from the car.

Gary started the engine and waited for Stephanie to get into the Volkswagen before he pulled out of the driveway.

It took only a few minutes to reach the Bridge of Lions, where Gary and Marian turned right to cross the bridge. Tapping the horn, Stephanie waved at them and continued up San Marco Avenue, which led to Highway 1 North into Jacksonville and the interstate toward Tallahassee. She threaded her way slowly through the downtown traffic, a frown creasing her forehead.

Marian had begun to deal with her feelings so soon after they had gotten home from the hospital, Stephanie thought, and over the past couple of weeks, she had become progressively calmer, steadier. There was still her anger at Talbot, of course, and that would continue to simmer until he was out of their lives. But it was a healthy anger, Stephanie knew, that Marian could keep in perspective and not allow to consume her. Neither of them kidded themselves about the after-effects of the attack; it would be a long time before the healing process would be complete. Still, Marian *had* begun the process that would bring her out on the other side — not only whole, but probably stronger as well.

Stephanie, however, had not allowed her deepest feelings of pain and rage at her own powerlessness to surface. It was as though she had bottled it up, she thought. She was saving it for Talbot.

She pushed the self-analysis aside, and the frown vanished. The coldness crept into her chest again, and she felt the corners of her mouth pull downward. She refused to look in the rearview mirror, knowing what she would see there. She had seen it that morning in the dresser mirror as she had turned to pick up her lighter. It had been the face of a stranger. It had been a face filled with such coldness and hardness that her hands had begun trembling with the knowledge of what was buried in the darkness inside of her.

Perhaps, she thought, the coldness would not have gained so

much control if she had not seen Talbot again.

But she had seen him.

Three days after she and Marian had returned from the hospital, Gary had been over for lunch. He had just left, and Stephanie was standing in the living room, looking out the window. A helmeted motorcyclist rolled past the house, slowed, and then continued to the cul-de-sac and turned around. Preoccupied at the time with thoughts totally unrelated to Talbot, she merely felt an uneasiness at first. But as the biker turned at the end of the street and came back, her uneasiness grew, and she suddenly felt faint as she sensed his presence.

Then the coldness had crept in.

She had not told Marian about the incident.

She told herself that by the time the police could have been alerted, Talbot would have disappeared again, and there was no need for Marian to be upset when nothing could be gained by it. That she might be rationalizing her refusal to tell Gary — that she might have hidden motives for that refusal — was a thought she continued to push to the back of her mind so she didn't have to deal with it.

Over the days since that first time, Talbot had grown bolder as his frustration grew at not being able to get to them easily. The frequent police surveillance of their house, combined with Gary's visits after dark, were working against him. But he could not contain his need to prove his lack of fear. She had seen him again, just a week ago, cruising past the house on the motorcycle.

And then yesterday.

She and Marian had come out of the small shop, and she had spotted him across the Plaza, although his back had been to them. Marian had gotten into the car, and Stephanie was opening her door when her attention was drawn, tugged at. Puzzled, she had swept her gaze across the expanse of the grassy square, past the Old Market, and back. And there he stood, seemingly attracted by the figures in the windows of Potter's Wax Museum.

He turned slowly, a mocking smile on his face. For one long moment, their eyes acknowledged one another across the Plaza.

But by that time, she no longer felt afraid. An icy hatred had absorbed it.

And because of that hatred, that coldness, she had deliberately lied to Marian for the first time.

At the Castillo de San Marcos, she turned right into the crowded parking lot and patiently waited until the dozen or so tourists with cameras trooped in front of the car without looking. Then she turned left out of the exit and headed back the way she had come.

He would know soon that she was alone.

Cat and mouse, she thought. *Cat and mouse.* The phrase played across her mind like a dark litany.

Tonight, or tomorrow at the latest, he would come for her. There would be nothing to stop him now. Even if he had wanted them both, he wouldn't pass up the opportunity to get her alone.

Cat and mouse. The words began to be a high-pitched squeal in her head.

Then, in a slower, heavier rasp. *Kill the bitch.*

She felt her eyes, her mouth grow harder, even icier.

This time, she would be ready for him.

She opened the glove compartment and took out the brown paper bag with the gun in it.

2

"A-1-A? What are you, a masochist?"

"I usually try to hide it," Marian said drily, but the corners of her mouth twitched with a smile. "What do you want to do — take the interstate all the way to Lauderdale?"

"Well—"

"Definitely *not*. This is what's called stopping to smell the flowers. We might even catch a glimpse of the *real* Florida from time to time on the coastal highway."

Gary grinned. "Yeah, I guess you're right. It'll make a nice drive."

They were silent then until they slowed for the heavy traffic making its way through Daytona Beach some thirty miles further down the coast. It had been a companionable trip so far, Marian thought, and she felt comfortable with the silence, but Gary seemed to have something on his mind. She tapped him on the shoulder.

"Hey, friend, what's going on?"

"Hmm?" He looked out the window, appearing to study the throng of sandal-footed vacationers who swarmed across the street in front of them.

"You've got that look that says you want to say something but you don't know how to say it."

"Are you sure Stephanie's the psychic?"

"No — actually, I talk and Stephanie moves her mouth." Marian smiled. "We considered a vaudeville act, but we found out that vaudeville's not around any more and TV wasn't ready for it."

Gary grinned, then he sobered slightly. "Well, I've been wanting to ask you a personal question. Do you mind?"

"If I do, I'll let you know."

"Fair enough," he grinned. "The question is — your friends. I've only seen Karen and Bob Fowler so far. Do you — that is, do you have other friends — gay friends?"

Marian raised an eyebrow. "Goodness, that *is* a terribly personal question."

Gary's face reddened. "Look, if I'm being stupid, just forget—"

"No. I'm sorry. Really." She patted his arm. "Of course we have gay friends. But Saint Augustine is not exactly the gay center of the world and, also, Stephanie and I have been fairly private people for the past few years. We used to be more involved politically — and, consequently, socially — but I suppose we started getting more wrapped up in our careers and more immediate things and we let that slip away for a while." She smiled as she saw Gary's intense frown of concentration. He wanted to understand everything at once, she thought, and it was clearly going to take more than one conversation about the matter. She shifted so she could face him and laid her arm on the back of the seat.

"We have friends in Villano Beach we see occasionally. An older male couple in Jacksonville. We make time to get to women's events from time to time, and once in a while, we even get to Atlanta, where we absolutely *wallow* in lesbians." She chuckled at his startled expression. "Figuratively speaking, of course." She pointed to the traffic light, which had turned green while he had his attention on her, then she frowned and shifted her gaze back to the street. "But the truth is also that since this — this *thing* started happening, we've kept more to ourselves because we didn't want to involve our friends in it."

Gary flinched, and Marian sighed at him. "You and Stephanie should form a club."

He glanced at her. "What?"

"Guilt and Regret Hoarders Not-So-Anonymous. She'd be the president, but you'd be in line for the second office. No contest."

"What does that mean?"

"Gary, you do all you can, and what you can't do, you forgive yourself for. Over and over and over, if need be."

"And I suppose you can do that all the time?" There was an edge to his voice.

"No." Marian stared out the window at the motels and gift shops that seemed to jostle and push each other for room on the street. "Sometimes it's very hard to do that."

Gary's tone was softer. "Sorry. I didn't mean to bring up—"

Marian smiled slightly. "Maybe I was getting a little preachy."

Gary cleared his throat. "Well, back to the other subject then?"

"Okay."

"Well, I heard what you said to Stephanie about this Julie. Is jealousy a problem?"

Marian grinned. "Not really. I suppose we got over that after a while, although if either of us is getting what may seem to be undue attention, the other might feel a twinge. But it's natural, and we usually get it out in the open and end up laughing about it."

"Even this Julie?"

"Julie," Marian laughed, "is someone I feel only a *very* little pinprick about. She *is* an attractive woman. And, Stef and she *were* lovers about ten years ago."

"It sounds like there's something more."

"You do your profession proud, my friend." Marian smiled, but she hesitated a moment.

"Have I finally crossed the line of too personal?"

"Well, I was wondering about that. But actually, if you asked Stephanie about it, I'm sure she'd tell you." She settled back against the seat again.

"Julie, you see, is rather the mystical type. She's really a sweetheart, but I have a hard time communicating with her. We seem to be at opposite ends of the belief spectrum. For Julie, everything that happens is related to the stars, the numbers, karma, whatever. I don't discount those things, but I give them a pretty hard look. Stephanie is probably somewhere in the middle. I suppose we assume that some of the metaphysical explanations for life are true, but until we know something definite, all we've really got to work with is this world."

"So is that what happened to them? Sort of a difference in perspective?"

"Well, no, not exactly," she grinned, "although ultimately I guess that had something to do with it. Julie and Stef met at a conference on psychic phenomena. Stephanie had already made a name for herself, and Julie thought she had found Mecca — her own private guru and psychic, all rolled up into one person. However, she discovered soon enough that Stephanie had a rather more psychological bent, and disillusionment set in."

"A monkey wrench in the works, I would expect."

"Mmm. Anyway, not long afterwards, Julie got the idea that in order to get off the karmic wheel — in other words," she said, seeing his look of puzzlement, "to avoid being born into another physical lifetime — all she had to do was practice celibacy."

"Oh." Gary's eyebrows lifted.

"Uh-oh is more like it. As Stephanie puts it, she was not particularly overjoyed at the news."

"So Stephanie left her."

"No, no, dear, I don't think that's in her nature. Really, she was very understanding. I think maybe she thought Julie would be amenable to discussing it at some point. She even went with Julie that summer on her annual trek to a spiritual retreat up in Vermont. That particular year, though, somebody who was a real fanatic on the subject got hold of Julie and convinced her that it would be better if she lived alone. Less temptation, I suppose, or—" She stopped abruptly.

"What's wrong?"

"That conference." Marian frowned. "Gary," she said slowly, "that conference is the third week in August. I know it is because Stef said something back in June about our going to see Julie then. She called her, and Julie said she wouldn't be in town because of a retreat."

"So maybe she didn't go."

"No. It's like a goddamned pilgrimage to her." She worried at her bottom lip for a minute, and when she spoke again, her voice was hard, the words clipped. "Julie is in Vermont. Right now. Stephanie didn't go to Tallahassee." She pointed to a phone booth outside a pastel-blue, stucco motel in the next block. "Stop there. Please."

As Gary pulled in, Marian threw open the car door and jumped out before the car had stopped completely. He watched as she made a call, hung up and made another one. When she slid back into the car, her fists were clenched.

"Stephanie's not at home. Neither is Julie."

Gary shrugged. "So she's on her way. She forgot Julie's trip, and she'll find out and go on to Tallahassee."

"*No.*" The anger in Marian's voice mounted, along with the fear. "She talked with Julie last week. She would have asked about staying then. She wouldn't have just popped in. So she knew. Damn it, she *knew.*" Marian hit the dashboard with her fist. "She either thought *I'd* forget — and I would have if we hadn't been talking about it — or she forgot herself when she lied to me."

"But what would she be doing, for God's sake?"

Marian stared out the windshield as if she were looking at something that was a long distance away. Her voice was quiet. "She's waiting for him."

"What?" The disbelief in his voice was unabashed.

Marian turned and looked at him, her eyes flashing with unconcealed anger now. "*She is waiting for him, goddamn it!* She must know when he's going to make his next move. And if I know her, she's probably making herself very conspicuous right now so he won't be able to miss the fact that she's alone."

Gary stared at her briefly, then he muttered something under his breath so softly that she could not hear it. He wrenched the car door open.

"I'll get somebody over there," he said.

They pulled up in front of the house behind a patrol car. A uniformed police officer who was leaning against the car pushed himself upright. Stephanie's car was in the driveway.

"When did she get back, Henry?"

"She was here when I pulled in, Sergeant. She asked me to wait outside."

Gary turned to Marian, who had taken her suitcase out of the trunk. "Do you want me to—"

"No. We need to be alone for a while." She slammed the trunk lid and strode toward the house.

As she opened the front door, she saw Stephanie sitting on the sofa, a brown paper bag in her lap. The room was dark, silent. Stephanie looked up, her face drawn, haggard.

Marian put the suitcase down and closed the door. Her hands shook. She studied Stephanie for a long time before she spoke, and when she did, her voice was a harsh whisper between clenched teeth.

"*Goddamn you,* Stephanie. How dare you do this. How *dare* you do this!"

Stephanie sighed heavily and placed the bag on the sofa beside her. Her eyes met Marian's.

"Do you want to know—"

"Christ, *no!* You don't have to tell me what you were doing!" Marian made an angry, sweeping gesture that encompassed the room. "You were waiting here like some goddamned sitting duck for him to walk in and kill you! *That's* what you were doing! *Damn* you, Stephanie!" Tears sprang suddenly into her eyes, and she wiped them away with a shaking hand. "You had some crazy idea about taking care of it yourself, didn't you? Like always. Well, *this* time, it just won't wash. What were you going to do — wait until he was at the fucking door — or maybe in the fucking house — and *then* call the police?"

Stephanie looked at Marian for a moment longer, then she took the gun from the bag and placed it on the coffee table in front of her.

The silence in the room had grown thick, oppressive, when the heavy .38 thudded dully on the wood.

Marian stared at the gun and then at Stephanie.

"My God, Stef," she whispered. "Were you going to kill him?"

"Yes." It was a flat, expressionless statement, and Stephanie's eyes were dull.

Marian watched as Stephanie picked up the gun and shoved it back into the bag. A puzzled frown touched Marian's forehead. "How long have you been planning this?"

"Since the day after it happened."

"But that was over two weeks ago."

"It took a while to arrange it. I didn't want to lie to you, but you wouldn't leave."

Marian turned and faced the fireplace, her back to Stephanie. She leaned on the mantel for a moment before she turned to look at Stephanie again. Her voice was calm, but it was a controlled calm.

"Stef. I know you only meant to do what you thought you had to do. What you thought was best. But we've *got* to be together in this. You can't keep things from me. I mean it. I know I've been scared, and until it's over, I'm *going* to be scared. But the fear isn't as important as the trust is. If we don't have the trust any more, then we don't have much."

Stephanie reached for a cigarette on the coffee table. She didn't speak until she had it lit, and then she stared across the room, past Marian. Her voice was distant, as if she were speaking to a stranger. "Perhaps you're right. Maybe it would be better if we weren't together."

"What?"

"I said—"

"I *heard* what you said. I just don't know what you mean."

Stephanie stood, went to the window, and looked out. Her back was stiff, her shoulders tight. "I mean," she said slowly, "if you don't feel there's very much there any more, then it would be better if we — parted." The last word sounded strangled as it entered the stillness of the room.

Marian said nothing, and the silence seemed to press in until it was almost a shimmering presence. Ordinary sounds that would have gone unnoticed the day before suddenly seemed almost unbearably loud. The faucet in the kitchen sink dripped noisily. A neighbor's dog barked.

Marian frowned in the darkened silence. "You're not serious."

"Yes. I am. I think you'd be better off with Gary."

Marian passed her hand over her eyes. "What? What are you talking about?"

"He's in love with you." Stephanie's voice was still flat. "He can offer you something. Respectability, a home. You've always wanted a child. He can give you one. I can't. You'd be better off with him."

A car door slammed somewhere down the block.

Marian's voice quavered. "That's ridiculous, Stef. I have what I want with you. Home is where *we* are, and where anything else is concerned—"

"No. It's not ridiculous. I want you to leave."

The faucet dripped again.

"You want me to leave you."

"Yes."

Marian watched Stephanie across the room. When she finally spoke, her voice had calmed again.

"I don't believe you. I *won't* believe you until you look at me when you say it."

The faucet dripped.

And after another long, interminable minute, Stephanie's back seemed to wilt. Her shoulders drooped. She turned slowly and put the cigarette out in the ashtray on the table. Her cheeks were wet with tears, and her voice was harsh, ragged.

"You know I can't do that."

Marian closed the distance between them, and her arms went around Stephanie, whose body was shaking now. Her own eyes filled with tears. "God," she whispered, "I hoped you couldn't."

Stephanie cried then, long, hard sobs, and Marian moved her to the sofa, where they sat for slow, pain-filled minutes, Stephanie's head cradled against Marian's breast while Marian rocked her back and forth. As the sobs subsided, Stephanie took a deep, shuddering breath and wiped her face with her hands. Her voice held a trace of hardness even then.

"I won't let him hurt you again."

"Let the police take care of it, sweetheart."

"They didn't take care of it before. And I didn't, either."

Marian sighed and leaned back. She tugged at Stephanie until Stephanie was lying on her back with her head in Marian's lap. Marian looked down at her and smoothed the short hair back from the damp forehead.

"Stef," she said gently, "it happened. It wasn't your fault. If it was anyone's fault besides that maniac's, it was mine for going back into the house alone. All we can do now is go on."

Stephanie closed her eyes, and a tear trickled from the corner of her eye toward her ear. Tenderly, Marian wiped it away.

When Stephanie spoke again, her voice was quiet, intense. "You can trust me this time. I promise you that."

"Stef—"

But Stephanie seemed to measure out her words carefully, one by one, as if she were a child counting out pennies from a piggy-bank. "I will not let him hurt you again."

Marian held Stephanie's head closer to her body and closed her eyes. She nodded her head in resignation. "Yes," she said quietly. "I know you won't."

Silent minutes passed. Marian sat and held Stephanie in her arms.

Finally, Stephanie spoke. "I know where he is," she said softly. "Why we couldn't find him."

"Oh?"

"I've seen him twice now."

Marian nodded her head again, as if the revelation was something she had been waiting for, had been expecting to hear.

"We weren't thinking the way he was," Stephanie said.

"Hmm?"

"What did we assume he was doing?"

Marian gave a small shrug. "Well, I guess we assumed he ditched the car in Houston, then stole another one and drove back here."

"Right. And?"

"So he got back here and holed up in some motel."

"Except that we couldn't find him."

"Mmmm."

"Money to live on?"

"Maybe he had some — which seems doubtful. Or he'd have to get a job. He'd be taking too big a chance if he committed a lot of robberies around here, mugged people or whatever. Too much risk."

"So we figured he had to find a place to live and somewhere to get money that wouldn't lead the police to him."

"Seems logical."

Stephanie reached over and got another cigarette from the coffee table. Marian picked up the lighter and lit it for her. Stephanie dragged deeply and stared at the ceiling.

"Well, that's what threw us off. We weren't allowing for enough possibilities. You know we kept wondering why I'd feel he was one place and then he wouldn't be there?"

"I seem to recall that." Marian smiled.

Stephanie caught Marian's eyes. "The whole point was that he *was* somewhere else. Anywhere he wanted to be. But he wasn't moving around from motel to motel or whatever." She paused and flicked ashes into the ashtray. "What he was doing was moving the place. A van, camper, that kind of thing. He's got a motorcycle on the back. That way, even if he's spotted, nobody would know about the camper." She watched Marian's eyebrows lift.

"Jesus H. Christ," Marian breathed softly.

Stephanie nodded. "I think I even passed him that day he attacked you. Just when I got off the bridge. I was almost overcome by this sense of — evil. It's a wonder I didn't run right into the doll place. He apparently got the motorcycle later. But I didn't put the whole thing together until that morning at the hospital."

"Then that's how he was able to get money. He could rob a store in Orlando, mug somebody in Gainesville — maybe even in Georgia. That way, scarcely any notice would be attracted to him in terms of a pattern."

"Exactly."

"You must be right. My God," Marian said softly, "it would be perfect."

"Yes. Perfect." Stephanie turned over and flicked ashes off the cigarette again. "Almost."

"Almost?"

" 'Almost' because we know, and we're not supposed to."

Marian was quiet. She studied Stephanie, then she looked toward the window. Gary was standing by the patrol car still talking with the officer he had called Henry. She saw him glance toward the house, his brow furrowed. She looked down at Stephanie.

"There's really no other way to stop him, is there?" she said softly.

Stephanie looked up at her. "I don't think so." She stared at the tip of the cigarette. "I want you to leave."

Marian shook her head firmly. "No. If you're going to do this, I'll be with you when you do it."

"Marian—"

"No. There's no point in discussing it any further."

Stephanie sighed finally and nodded.

Marian looked toward the window again. "He'll never agree to it."

"He'll have to," Stephanie said quietly.

3

"What is it?" Marian lay the book down on her sheet-covered stomach and took off her glasses.

Stephanie stood beside the bed and smoothed lotion onto her hands. She seemed to be looking into the distance, her eyes unfocused, staring into nothingness.

"Beam me up, Scottie," Marian said. "There's no intelligent life down here."

Stephanie started, then she laughed softly as she allowed the remark to sink in. But a frown replaced the smile quickly.

"I've been thinking. Maybe I've been kidding myself all these years. I've always thought of myself as — as a caring person, understanding. Maybe I'm not. Maybe I've been covering up something — just pretending. Not seeing what I really am."

Marian picked up her glasses and chewed thoughtfully on one earpiece while she studied Stephanie. "What do you think you've been covering up?"

Stephanie screwed the cap on the hand-lotion bottle and pushed it to the back of the night table. "I don't know really. But for the first time, I'm aware of a very cold place deep inside of me."

Marian smiled tenderly. "Like the little voice in the scary place?"

"Maybe." She sighed. "I keep thinking about my sister. How I hurt her. Maybe that's who I really am."

Marian frowned. "Who you really are? You mean, maybe you're really a terrible person and you've just been pretending all this time."

"Yes." Stephanie shed the bathrobe and slipped into bed. She pulled the sheet up over her breasts and folded her hands on her stomach. Marian continued to study her.

"Let me get this right," Marian finally said, her voice holding a tinge of teasing in it. "All these years — ever since you were nine years old — you've really been a killer at heart." She furrowed her brow into a frown of mock concentration. "Even though you haven't killed anyone, of course. But you've just put on this mask of a kind, loving, considerate person. Is that anything close to what you mean?"

Stephanie shot her a sharp look. "Are you making fun of me?"

Marian smiled gently and patted Stephanie's intertwined hands. "A little," she said softly. "I'm sorry, honey, but it doesn't happen that way. And you know that. If one of your clients said what you just have, you could see it. If you were walking around covering up that kind of — well, evil, let's call it, then you'd be aware of it all the time. You'd have to consciously deceive people."

"What about—"

"No," Marian said with firmness. "I don't mean your lying to me, either. In fact, that's just an additional argument in my favor. You did that out of love. You believed you had to protect me. And that's the whole point. I don't believe that anyone who is as cold as you're talking about would be able to love anyone the way you love me."

"Even killers can love someone else."

"No. It's not the same thing. Somebody who kills — or at least somebody who kills without feeling anything about it — sees the love object as only that. An object. I'm not sure that's love. It may be need or dependence or whatever, and we all have some of that — but it's not a giving kind of love like you feel for me." She shook her head. "No, dear, I'm sorry, but you just don't fit the description of a cold-blooded killer."

Stephanie sighed. "I don't know. If that's not inside of me, then how could I have done that to my sister?"

"You were a child, Stef. You were not capable of controlling that mental energy then."

Stephanie rubbed her eyes. "You don't understand."

"I understand that you're still tormenting yourself for something you did more than thirty years ago. Besides which, you don't even remember everything that happened. Frankly, I suspect —"

Stephanie's voice was hard, intense. "I remember reaching into her mind and then seeing her cower in a corner, crouching on the floor. I remember her eyes staring vacantly and her screaming going on and on. I remember that very well."

"But you don't remember what happened before that. Stef, she probably had some element of the same kind of power you have. She just couldn't handle it — or it manifested itself in her in a different way. Maybe she was already mentally or emotionally disturbed because of it. Something — I don't know what — but something happened inside her head, and she picked up a knife and came at you. You defended yourself."

"I didn't have to do that to her."

"You had to *survive*, damn it. And you even waited until she hurt you. Why do you think you have that scar, Stef?"

Stephanie's mouth was set in a tight line. "All I know is that my sister is still in a mental institution in Boston, and that my mother has spent the last thirty years of her life taking care of her. I know that I stopped going to see her twenty years ago because every time I went into that room she would start screaming and banging her head against the wall. *That I know.*"

Marian rubbed her forehead in frustration, then she took a deep breath and let it out slowly. "Well, I don't know for sure about your sister, Stef. But I know that you're not a terrible person. That's what *I* know. And I know that each of us has a survival instinct. I think that's the cold place you're talking about. It's what therapists like to call the dark side. And we touch it, I think, when we're angry or hurt or afraid. We feel threatened, and we strike out." She caressed Stephanie's hands. "Right now, your very life is being threatened, and the life of someone you love. It's natural for you to feel what you're feeling. And given that, I have to believe that where your sister is concerned, you were threatened, and you struck out to protect yourself."

"Frank Talbot kills people who are no threat to him." Her voice was emotionless.

"Well, we all feel threat to ourselves in different ways, Stef. What I perceive as a threat to myself, you may not. And vice versa. Frank Talbot probably sees threats to himself from any number of directions. The way somebody says something to him, the way somebody looks at him. Constantly. Sometime, very long ago, perhaps he closed himself off entirely in order not to be hurt any more. Now, he hurts someone else before they can become a threat to him so he doesn't have to deal with being hurt."

"I closed myself off a long time ago, too," Stephanie whispered. "Maybe I did the same thing he did."

Marian grimaced. "You have to struggle constantly to close yourself off, Stephanie. Your natural state is to be open and loving."

"Maybe his is, too, and he just got trapped in that other side. Sometimes I feel trapped, too. Maybe we all have experiences we can't get past."

"If you believed that, you couldn't do counseling — and neither could I. People are responsible for their lives. They can change. Or they can choose not to." She sighed heavily. "And I grant you the dichotomy. Perhaps we are, at times, incapable of choosing change because of certain experiences. But we are *still* responsible." She waved her hand in a gesture of weariness. "And that gets you to existential despair. The basic isolation of the individual and the idea that maybe everything is out of our control — and yet we're still responsible for even that." She turned over on her side and held Stephanie's eyes for a moment. "But you can't live your life out of that, and you know it. Because it may *not* be true."

"But if it *is* true — then maybe we're all trapped. Maybe I'm just like Frank Talbot."

Marian's voice became an intense whisper. "You are *not* like Frank Talbot. The very fact that you — at a time when you would *naturally* hate his guts — are actually considering the pain *he* might have experienced in his life, is proof enough. Can't you see that?"

Stephanie looked into Marian's eyes and then shifted her gaze across the room again. "If that's true," she said softly, "we might have more to worry about than I had thought."

"What do you mean?"

"I can't afford to think about his pain right now." She shook her head. "Later, maybe. But not now."

Part
Five

1988

Monday

17

August

1

"No." Gary shook his head firmly. "No, it's insane. Absolutely insane." He dumped another spoonful of sugar into his coffee and stirred it so vigorously that some spilled over into the saucer. "And I can't believe that you've known all of this for two weeks and haven't told me. I ought to arrest you for withholding evidence or obstructing justice."

Marian laughed quietly. "It would probably be the first time a psychic was arrested for knowing something most people wouldn't believe she could know in the first place."

Gary muttered under his breath before he looked at her again. "Unfortunately, you're right." The spoon clattered noisily against the saucer as he laid it down. "But I can't go along with this crazy scheme of yours."

Marian sighed and rolled her eyes at Stephanie, who had been sitting quietly while Marian argued with him.

"Gary," Stephanie said, her voice reflecting a patient weariness, "we cannot continue to live like this. We've got to do something, and this is the only way we know to do it. He's not going to make his move as long as he sees the police crawling all over the place. He'll just wait until you're gone."

"Then I'll have a woman officer stay here at night. It would be too risky for him to do anything during the day again."

Marian took an exasperated breath and huffed it out. She gave Stephanie a look that said, "Do you believe this?", then she turned her attention back to Gary. "Christ. I don't think you've been listening at all! The point is not that he won't make a move while a *man* is around — and, incidentally, I resent the implication—"

"Sorry."

She waved off the apology. "The point is, as long as we're not *alone*, he's not going to do anything."

"And what he'll do, damn it, is come in here and *kill* both of you!" He slammed his palm on the table and glared at her.

Marian leaned back in the chair and shook her head as if she had become tired of the fight.

Stephanie studied him for a minute. "Listen, Gary, I'll know when he's coming this time. We'll call you, and you'll get somebody here right away."

"I don't like it."

Marian's eyes flashed with anger. "It's not entirely up to you."

Stephanie tapped a cigarette on the edge of the table and lit it before she looked at him again. "How long do you think you'll be able to keep a stakeout alive?" she said quietly.

"What?"

"Sooner or later, regardless of what you say about it — or what *we* say — your superiors will make you drop it. It seems to me that it would be easier to make Talbot think he can do something now. So we can get it over with."

Gary stood, walked stiffly to the stove, and poured more coffee. "I can persuade them to let me keep somebody posted as long as necessary."

"I hear your ego talking," Marian said.

They glared at each other for a moment, and Marian finally softened. "I'm sorry. That was unfair." Gary accepted the apology with a shrug.

"We have to get this over with, Gary, so Stephanie and I can go on with our lives. If the only object is for us to be safe, we could hire an armed guard to live with us for the rest of our lives. Or you could lock us up. We'd be safe then. *Maybe.* But we're not willing to do that. We have to take this risk in order to be free of him."

Gary sat down again and sipped at the coffee. He avoided Marian's eyes. At last, he took a deep breath and let it out in an exaggerated sigh of resignation, then he turned toward Stephanie.

"I suppose you know how he'll do it?"

"From the back. The inlet."

"The inlet."

"Mmm."

"How in hell do you know that?"

"I suppose because he's come up with a plan now, because I get a very clear sense of danger coming from there." She paused. "Actually, he must have done that before. Maybe not from the inlet, but from the back of the house. The day he killed Mr. Pye. That day, I felt something when Marian and I were in the backyard. I just wasn't putting it together then."

"So I post somebody back there."

Stephanie shook her head. "No. It won't work. If there's even a chance he'll see you, it's no good."

"You're not making this easy." He rubbed at his eyes with the heels of his hands. "Okay. I'll put an unmarked car up the street a couple of blocks and put a listening device in the house." He looked at Stephanie and then at Marian with eyebrows lifted in a sarcastic expression. "I assume that meets with your approval so far?"

Marian grimaced at him.

"I just don't like it," he repeated.

Stephanie looked at Marian. Marian was staring at the faucet dripping in the sink.

"Gary," Stephanie said quietly, "it will be okay."

He studied her. "That sounds like you know something else I don't."

"I'm just saying it will be all right. You don't have to worry."

He looked at Marian, but she avoided his eyes. She sat stiffly and stared at the faucet.

"What *is* this?"

Stephanie sighed. Then she met his eyes and very slowly, very carefully, she extended her consciousness toward him. She could feel herself sitting in her chair, but a part of her mind began to touch his, tenuous mental fingers parting strands of his mind, his memories. She walked through his past, opening a door here, a door there, looking into all the darkened rooms. Finally she found the door she wanted and flooded with a soft light the room she had entered. The part of her that remained in the chair watched his eyes widen. After a minute or so, she saw him put his hand to his forehead, his eyes puzzled. And then she felt the hint of fear that began to seep down the corridors of his mind. Before it could grow, she withdrew — slowly, carefully, gently. She closed the mental door and left the way she had come. Breaking the connection, she felt her consciousness spill completely back into her own body, and she took a deep breath and let it out.

"My God," he said softly. "What did you do?"

"What did it feel like?"

"I — I don't know." He looked at Marian, but she was still staring ahead. "It felt sort of like a hand, I suppose. Like you put your hand inside my head. There was this—" He struggled with the words. "Like there was something — holding my mind, I guess. I started thinking about Jenny all of a sudden. It was almost as if we were in the house we used to live in. The first night we were together. Not like I was remembering it really, but like I was there. Like I was really there," he repeated softly. His eyes misted slightly, and he rubbed at them quickly and cleared his throat to cover his embarassment. He picked up the cup, and his hand trembled. "Then I felt — afraid — a feeling of being out of control, I suppose. I mean, if you had wanted to, you could have—" He glanced at her in sudden comprehension, and his voice grew even softer. "That's it, isn't it? You could do that to Talbot."

"Yes." Stephanie crushed out the cigarette in the ashtray and avoided his eyes for several seconds. "I could stimulate something in his mind that would produce fear."

Gary's tone belied his excitement then, and his eyes glittered briefly. Stephanie looked away, not wanting to see what seemed to be an almost triumphant gleam in his expression. She had seen the look before, when people who had felt powerless began to sense their own power over others. It was natural, she knew, for Gary to feel it in this situation. But it was still hard to watch it dawn in his eyes. It was an emotion she had fought against within herself for most of her life.

"If you pushed him — I mean *really* pushed him," Gary said with sharp intensity, "what would be the most you could do?"

"It depends. I suppose he could literally die of fear. If his heart was weak enough, which it probably isn't." She lit another cigarette and met his eyes again. "But the most likely result would be insanity. Briefly, anyway." She paused. "Assuming I could do it."

"But it's obvious you can do it."

Stephanie shook her head slightly. "Not necessarily. I mean, if you knew I was going to do that to you again, you'd be able to block me to some degree — hold me off. And besides," she said, her voice cool, "I do have a few qualms about doing that to another human being, you know."

"But you could—"

Suddenly Marian seemed to come out of her trance, and her voice had a sharp, hard edge to it. "No."

Stephanie jerked her head toward her. "Marian, we agreed that—"

"I've changed my mind. We can do something else."

"Why not?" Gary's disbelief raised his voice. "It would be self-defense. Besides that, it would even be assumed that he just flipped out."

"No," Marian repeated, her mouth set in a grim line.

Gary stared at her. "This is incredible. *He is trying to kill you.*"

"Yes, he is. And let's just say that Stephanie is not going to do that. She won't have to. You said yourself that you'll have somebody near."

"Well, no, I don't think it'll be necessary for Stephanie to follow through on it, but if it comes down to it—"

"No!"

"Well, why the fuck not!" Gary exploded.

"There's no point in discussing it any further," Marian said stiffly. Then she pushed her chair back, stood, and walked into the living room, slamming the door behind her.

Gary looked at Stephanie, his mouth open with surprise, but Stephanie was looking toward the closed door. She stood and followed Marian.

Marian stood in the middle of the living room, her arms hugged around herself. Stephanie came up behind and placed her hands on Marian's shoulders.

"I thought we had this worked out," she said quietly.

"I thought so, too. I guess I didn't."

"Marian, if it comes to that, I've got to do it."

Marian turned in Stephanie's arms and looked at her steadily. "I've seen what that did to you once. How much guilt do you think you can stand, Stef? This time you might destroy yourself with it. And it might even destroy *us*."

Stephanie bent her head. "I guess I'll only know that if it happens." She lifted her eyes again to Marian's. "I just know that I will do what I can if I have to."

There was a heavy silence in the room, broken only by their breathing. After a moment, Marian's shoulders fell in a gesture of surrender, and she put her arms around Stephanie and sank against her shoulder.

"I suppose you're right. I won't try to stop you."

"I need more than that," Stephanie said softly. "I need you to be with me all the way. I need you to believe that no matter what happens, we'll make it through."

Marian didn't move her head, and she was silent for a while. But finally, she nodded slightly.

"Yes," she whispered. "No matter what happens."

1988

Sunday

23

August

1

Talbot set the beer can down on the tiny fold-out table in the camper and studied the sixteen-year-old girl who bent over the rangetop.

"That smells like shit."

Her mouth dropped in that stupid look he hated, and her voice whined at him. "You wanted fried eggs. I'm fixin' them. The grease just got a little old is all."

He hated that whine. It had begun to grate on his ears like rusty gears two days ago. But he wouldn't have to hear it much longer. She'd served his purpose.

A fucking runaway he'd picked up hitchhiking a week before. He had wanted to get a piece of ass, and it had ended up costing him less than he'd expected — less than a whore would've ended up costing him. And he'd gotten a lot more use out of her than if he'd bought a whore for the night. Besides, she didn't eat much. He chuckled under his breath. Except what he wanted her to eat.

He watched as she poked her bottom lip out and blew limp, mousy-brown hair off her damp forehead. She scooped the eggs onto a paper plate with toast and slid it in front of him. Then she sat down across from him and propped her chin on her hands and looked at him hopefully.

The eggs stared up at him like two fat yellow eyes. One of them had broken and was running across the plate into the grease. The toast, made before the eggs had been cracked into the skillet, was cold, limp. He looked at it and shoved the plate back across the table. "This looks like pig slop. You're a pig. You eat it."

Her face contorted in that look he had come to despise. "Why you gotta talk to me that way, Frankie?" she whined nasally.

He hated the name. It made him sound like a kid. His whore of a mother had called him that.

In an explosion of movement, he stood up, picked up the plate, and slid the contents onto her head. She gasped and started crying and wiping at the mess that ran down her face and matted her hair. He grabbed a handful of hair, ignoring her surprised yelp, and jerked her head back. He glared into her reddening eyes. The tears mingled with the broken yellow eyes that ran down her babyish face.

"Go clean yourself up, pig," he hissed. Still clenching her hair in his fist, he lifted her out of the chair and pounded the side of a hard fist against her thigh. She yelled again, a wail of pain, and clutched at his hand. He jerked his hand away, clamped it over her mouth, and slammed her against the countertop.

"Shut up," he said, and his voice sounded all the more deadly for its quietness. "Unless you want more of what I gave you the last time."

Her eyes turned into huge round circles in her face then. She had limped for a whole day that time, and he knew she would do just about anything to avoid that. She nodded her head vigorously. When he released her, she scurried into the cubicle that was the bathroom at the back of the camper.

He stood there for a minute, then he washed the egg off his hands at the sink. As he dried them, he looked toward the door.

She had been more trouble than he had planned on.

He had stolen half a dozen vans and campers since he had crossed into Florida. It hadn't been that hard. Most of them had belonged to stupid tourists who left them parked at the rest areas along the interstate while they went in. He'd ditch the one he had close to the interstate, hike into the rest area, and watch for an unlocked one. Afterwards, he'd hit another rest area and find a van or camper that was backed into the parking space, and he would rip off the license plate. It was doubtful that the owner would even know it was missing for maybe hundreds of miles, unless a cop stopped them. And stealing a camper and putting another plate on it was safe. They would see one that had been reported stolen, but it would have a different plate. It had been working well. Easy as shit.

He had seen the girl the day after he had ripped off the camper they were in now, on his way back after he thought he finally had the bitch. He had been filled with rage, and he had wanted a woman.

Darlene had been standing at one of the exits onto the interstate. In just that flash, he had seen the sassy hip stuck out, the big tits jutting out at him, her thumb poking skyward. And getting her had been no trouble at all. None at all.

But after a while, he'd realized that all she meant was trouble. He'd have to get rid of her soon. Somebody had to be looking for her, and that could be dangerous. If they found her, she'd talk her stupid head off.

Talbot threw the towel over the rack beside the sink and turned as she came out of the bathroom toweling her hair, clad in a pair of scanty black panties he'd had her buy. Her breasts bounced up and down as her arms moved back and forth. When he reached to touch her, she shrank back, fear flooding her eyes again. But he smiled at her, and, a little hesitantly at first, she smiled back. Her smile grew broader as he closed one hand over a large breast. He pulled her to him as he leaned back against the counter and rubbed his thumb over the nipple. It hardened instantly. He pinched the other one, and she closed her eyes and sank against him.

An hour later, she turned from him during her sleep and began to snore. He reached under the pillow and closed his hand around the handle of the knife he had hidden there that morning.

Just after midnight, Talbot drove to the Saint John's River near Palatka, stopped on the bridge, and dragged her body to the railing. He heaved the body midway over the railing, and gases were expelled in a stench that made him gag for several seconds. Balancing her weight there, he picked up the concrete block that was tied to her ankles and dropped it over the railing. The body jerked free of the bridge and plummeted to the swirling black water below.

She would surface somewhere later, Talbot thought, as he wiped his hands hard on his jeans. But by that time, it wouldn't matter. Dead, she'd be no trouble to him at all.

"Are you sure you feel like reading?"

Stephanie turned a page in the book. "Just a little while longer," she murmured.

Marian snuggled closer and placed her hand on Stephanie's bare stomach under the sheet. "It's getting pretty late."

"Mmm." Stephanie continued to read, but she patted Marian's hand absentmindedly.

Marian studied Stephanie's face for a while, observing the still predominantly dark hair slanted across the forehead that was lined slightly in concentration. The silver-gray that dusted it now would soon gain the upper hand, she thought with a smile. Her eyes followed the curve of the hairline down and behind the small, delicate ears, traced with a mental finger the finely chiseled jawline, and frowned slightly as she reached the jagged scar that crossed the jaw — the scar that had left so much more pain in Stephanie's soul than on her face. It was a face, Marian considered, that was attractive in such a strong way that most people would call Stephanie a handsome woman — not pretty or beautiful, but handsome. And her body — still lean and strong, although there was definite gentling of the breasts, a bit more fat that had softened her belly and inner thighs — all changes that Marian had watched lovingly as they had taken place over the past eight years.

Marian caressed Stephanie's hip. In many ways, she mused, Stephanie's body brought her more pleasure now than in the beginning. A slight smile touched the corners of her mouth. If that was possible. As the months and then the years had gone by, their lovemaking had mellowed, of course, as they had mellowed in other ways. The newness had worn off after a while, and they had come to know each other's responses so well that, from time to time, it required a bit of attention to keep the romantic spark alive. But the love had grown, and there were still those memorable nights — and hot afternoons — when their need for each other summoned back that old excitement that took her breath away. Now, with this threat in their lives, the fear seemed to put a biting edge on even that hunger, imbuing it with a sense of urgency.

"Stef?" She pressed her body more insistently against

Stephanie's and watched as Stephanie studiously turned another page. "Are you teasing me?"

Stephanie raised her eyebrows at Marian. "Whatever could you mean?"

Marian raised herself on one elbow and stared into Stephanie's eyes. The little lines began to crinkle at the corners, and Stephanie's mouth twitched slightly, as though she were holding back a smile.

"Why, you bitch!" Marian exclaimed in mock outrage.

Stephanie grinned and put the book on the table, but as she turned back, she grasped Marian's wrists and pushed her back onto the bed, pinning her. Laughing, Marian turned her head when Stephanie tried to kiss her, and it was only after several seconds of playful struggle that Stephanie managed to grasp Marian's jaw with her free hand. She lowered her mouth to take the kiss, and Marian's laughter subsided as she finally ceased the struggle and gave herself to the demanding victor.

But just as Marian's breathing became more rapid and shallow under the slow, sensuous ministrations of the mouth on hers, Stephanie lifted herself slightly and gazed down at her willing captive. Marian lifted her head from the pillow to be kissed again, but Stephanie held her off now, the teasing smile once more touching her mouth. Finally, after a second attempt, Marian fell back onto the bed. She laughed softly and felt the familiar languidness take over her body.

"This feels like a very old game," Marian whispered.

"Does it?"

"Mmm. I feel like the heroine in a historical romance novel. Ravished by the conquering—" She grinned. "The conquering heroine." She moved seductively, heard the catch in Stephanie's breath and smiled. "There are times," she murmured, "when I want nothing more than to surrender totally to you. I lose all sense of my own will." Her smile turned to a small intake of breath as Stephanie's hand drifted to the inside of her thigh.

Stephanie continued the caress and queried, as though puzzled by the abrupt halt in Marian's side of the conversation, "You were saying?"

Marian's smile recurred fleetingly, then it disappeared into a soft gasp before she continued. "I was saying," she whispered raggedly, "that there are times when you could do anything with me you wanted to."

Stephanie laughed quietly. "Only because you let me."

"Sometimes I'm not so sure," Marian murmured. She closed her eyes and moved her hands slightly against the pressure of the hand that clasped hers so lovingly on the pillow above her head. It was a movement designed more to experience the sense of being captured than to try to escape. When she gave herself over to that experience, she felt safe, warm. But after a minute, she opened her eyes, moved provocatively again, and watched Stephanie's eyes grow dark, hungry, almost fierce with her want. As Stephanie bent to brush her lips across Marian's waiting mouth, Marian whispered, "Please. Let go of my hands." Stephanie complied, and Marian moved her hands out from Stephanie's and clasped the dark head above her. She moaned deeply in her throat as she felt Stephanie's hands begin their loving task in earnest.

Marian leaned over Stephanie and looked at the clock. "It's about midnight," she said. She felt Stephanie's hand slide down to her buttock and squeeze gently. "Don't get me started again," she whispered with a smile. "I already feel like a lewd, lascivious woman."

Stephanie chuckled. "I understand that in the face of danger, people's natural response is to grab as much of life as they can."

"That's not life, sweetheart," Marian grinned, "that's my ass." She snuggled down beside Stephanie and caressed the warm thigh beside hers. "I want to hear a Mother Goose story."

"Hmm?"

"You know how kids like to hear the same story over and over? The ones where the good people live happily ever after?"

"Mmm."

"It gives them a sense of security, I guess. The story's always the same. It never changes. The hideous troll under the bridge is defeated, and the happy couple walk hand-in-hand into the sunset." She turned her head on Stephanie's shoulder so she could look at her. "I'm suddenly scared again, Stef. You?"

Stephanie hugged her. "Me, too." She kissed the top of Marian's head. "I can tell you about one happy couple I know, but I don't have an ending to the story yet."

"That's okay. You can make one up." She caressed Stephanie's naked thigh. It was warm, and she knew if she moved her hand upwards just a little, she would find even warmer flesh that would be wet to her touch. "You'll be well repaid for your efforts."

"I thought I'd already been amply rewarded," Stephanie murmured.

Marian laughed softly in her throat. "Well, perhaps something a little different next time."

Stephanie fumbled on the night table in the dark for another cigarette, moving quietly, gingerly. Marian, curled beside her, shifted slightly in her sleep, mumbled something unintelligible, and smiled. Then she flopped over and stretched out on her side, facing away from Stephanie.

In the flame of the cigarette lighter, Stephanie caught a glimpse of Marian's back and hips as the sheet fell away when she turned. Her back was smooth, warmly tanned until just below her waist, where her bathing suit mark began. Her hips flared there, softly lit in the light of the flame, and curved gently into the rounded globes of her buttocks. Stephanie reached out and tenderly touched Marian's hip with the back of her hand. Even though the physical wounds from the attack had disappeared, she could still see them in her mind's eye. Marian murmured in her sleep again, and Stephanie clicked the lighter closed.

Without warning, Stephanie's eyes flooded with tears, but this time she did not try to stop them. After all the years they had been together, she thought, she was still achingly touched by Marian's gentleness and her strength, her caring and her passion. So much so that she felt helpless at times when she tried to tell Marian how she felt. After the years of loneliness before, she had finally found some one whose love for her seemed unbounded — someone who could not only forgive the silence, but who understood it as well.

And now, Stephanie agonized, if she made another mistake, she could repay that love with pain again — and this time, perhaps with death.

Stephanie sighed, wiped her eyes, and moved the cigarette to her lips. The tip glowed orange-red in the darkness. A breeze fluttered the curtains open. If they could have moved from Saint Augustine, she thought, and been assured that it would be over, she would have done it gladly, would have accepted the pain of separation from what had been her place of peace. They would have made a life together somewhere else. But somewhere deep inside, she knew it would be of no use to move. His rage would find them anywhere.

When she finished her cigarette, she stretched out, her belly against Marian's back. She curved an arm around Marian and held her firmly. Marian woke only slightly, found Stephanie's hand, and moved it to her breasts. She held it there, caressing it. Her voice was sleepy-soft in the silence.

"I love you," she mumbled.

Stephanie kissed the silky shoulder. "I love you, too," she whispered. She held Marian more closely.

They would not have much longer to wait.

1988

Friday

26

August

Frank Talbot propped up the folding mirror in front of him on the table and rubbed the back of his hand across his mouth. He unscrewed the jar of lampblack and slid the flat of his fingertips across its contents. Gingerly at first, he began to pat it on his face.

Just like Nam. Like the night before a raid.

After he had applied the lampblack, he leaned back in the folding chair and stared at his face in the mirror. He grinned and chugged the rest of the beer.

Soon.

It was so close now, it was hard to wait.

As darkness closed in that night, he abandoned the camper on a deserted road and began hiking up the coast, keeping well in the shadows.

1988

Saturday

27

August

Stephanie awakened slowly and stretched under the sheets. Noticing that the other side of the bed was empty and that the sun was not yet bright at the window, she turned over and looked at the clock. It was only a little after seven, but Marian was already up.

Yawning, she arose, belted her robe around her, and padded down the hall to the kitchen. Coffee was on the stove. Through the living room, she spotted Marian sitting on the front steps. She brushed her fingers through her hair and wandered back down the hall to the bathroom. A few minutes later, feeling considerably more awake, she poured a cup of coffee and went out to the porch.

Marian did not turn around as the screen door was opened behind her and Stephanie sat down on the steps.

"It's a beautiful morning, isn't it?" Marian said quietly.

"Yes, it is." Stephanie sipped at the coffee and looked around. It was cool. The early-morning sun filtering through the palms struck the lavender bougainvillea at the side of the yard. It would be hotter, but for the time being, the coolness could be savored even more because it would be fleeting. A blue jay called raucously from one of the mimosas, filling the silence with its cry.

Stephanie took one of Marian's hands, but still Marian did not turn. Her cheeks were wet with tears, and she wiped at them with her other hand.

"You know," Marian said, "it's so beautiful today, maybe we should go to the beach. We could take a picnic lunch. We haven't done that in a while."

"That would be nice."

There was a long silence then, and Stephanie put her arm around Marian's shoulders and drew her close. Marian sank against Stephanie, but she didn't speak.

"Marian?"

"Mmm?"

"You're pregnant, aren't you?"

Marian looked at Stephanie then, and a fresh flood spilled out of her eyes and down her cheeks. She nodded. "I think so," she said haltingly. "I thought at first it was just the stress. But that would have made me only a few days late — a week at most. Not this long." She laughed humorlessly. "I guess the so-called 'morning-after pill' didn't work." She looked down at Stephanie's hand and held it in both of hers. She rubbed her thumb gently across the knuckles, caressing it as though she had never seen it before.

"I've just been sitting here thinking." She turned Stephanie's hand over and ran her finger along the lines of the palm, then she placed her own palm against it and entwined their fingers. "Do you remember," she said softly, "that night a couple of years ago when we were making love — and afterwards I started crying because," she paused, "because I wanted to have your child?"

Stephanie squeezed Marian's hand tenderly. "Yes. I remember."

Marian made a small sighing sound. "I felt like my heart was going to break I wanted it so much. And I felt like such a fool." She began caressing Stephanie's hand again. "You were so understanding. You held me and cried with me, and I loved you so much I thought I might just disappear. It seemed like such a cruel thing that what I wanted was so impossible."

Stephanie said nothing for a moment, and when she finally spoke, her words were so soft that Marian had to strain to hear them. "I know," she said. "For me, too." She swallowed hard and blinked her eyes as if it could stop her tears. "Do you know how much I love you?" she asked in a whisper that caught in her throat.

Marian took Stephanie's face in her hands and held the dark eyes with her own. Pulling Stephanie toward her, she leaned forward and kissed her. It was a slow, warm, caressing kiss that lasted a long time, and when Marian drew back, she said softly, "Yes. I do. And I never get tired of hearing you say it."

Stephanie smiled shakily and nodded, then she cleared her throat and turned to pick up the cup of coffee. "Well," she started slowly, "we've talked about your having a child through artificial insemination, or maybe our adopting one."

"Mmm." Marian rested her hand on Stephanie's knee. "But we've always been so busy with work — and with each other. And it would've taken a lot of red tape to adopt a child." A certain bitterness appeared in her voice. "And now, it seems the child we are presented with is from the man who wants to kill us."

Stephanie sipped at her coffee and stared out at the yard again. "Heartfelt reaction," she said. "Not from your head." She paused. "Do you want this child?"

Marian shook her head and leaned back against the step. She rubbed Stephanie's back, then patted it. "I don't know." She stopped for a moment and then resumed, her voice holding a slight edge of hardness. "Yes. I do know. I don't want his child. I want yours."

Stephanie laughed tenderly. "And given that what we want is impossible?"

Marian closed her eyes. "I just don't know. I'm older now. The risk is greater. But I'm healthy, which can be placed on the positive side of the balance sheet. And there's my career. I doubt that a child would be much of a help to that at this point." She sighed. "And, of course, if it were your child, none of those things would be an issue at all. There would be no questions in my mind. I'd have it." She groaned. "Maybe I'm just trying to be rational about something I can't be rational about."

They sat for a moment without speaking, then Marian sighed again.

"You know, Stef, I guess the main thing I've been wondering about is — well, what if every time I looked at the child I thought of its father?"

"I think you could separate them. The child wouldn't be its father."

Marian shook her head. "I don't know." She looked at Stephanie's back. "And you — what about you, sweetheart? Could you raise a child — look at it every day — knowing it was here because its father raped me?"

Stephanie turned and looked at her steadily, silently.

"What is it, Stef?"

"It's not a simple yes or no answer."

Marian half-smiled. "It rarely is." She laid her hand on Stephanie's arm. "Maybe you'd better tell me what you're feeling. Better now than later."

Stephanie pulled a pack of cigarettes from the pocket of her bathrobe and lit one, taking a great deal of time doing so. She inhaled deeply before she spoke.

"I'm considering two things. One. Even though I wouldn't blame the child, I don't know if I'll ever be able to forgive Talbot for what he did to you."

"That sounds honest."

"But that's been out in the open for quite a while."

"Mmm. And there's something else that hasn't been out in the open?"

"Maybe." Stephanie frowned. "I guess there's something else floating around somewhere that wonders . . . " Her voice was tight, as if she were dragging words out that were resisting her attempt to expose them. "If I let go of my hatred of him — I might feel that I was being disloyal to you." She turned to look at Marian.

Marian's eyebrows lifted, and she exclaimed softly, "God, Stef, that hadn't even occurred to me." She rubbed Stephanie's arm and was silent for a minute. "Sweetheart, neither of us is going to be able to deal with our anger against him — that is, letting go of it — until this thing is over. I'd like to think we could, but I'm not sure it's humanly possible. But eventually, we're both going to have to because it's too destructive a thing to carry around for very long." She smiled. "Although I must confess that if you didn't feel so strongly, I might wonder a little."

Stephanie grinned. "*That* sounds honest."

Marian became quiet and began caressing Stephanie's arm again. "You know, one thing that men deal with after their wives — lovers — are raped is that most of them feel something has been taken from them." She gave a slight shrug and seemed to be studying

Stephanie's arm in detail, avoiding her eyes.

"Yes, but that's. . ."

"Let me finish, honey." Marian frowned. "That's why I said that about how you would feel when you looked at the child, knowing his father had raped me. The point is, they feel somebody's spoiled something for them. They're trained to see women as their possessions, and that's where part of their anger comes from. It's as if somebody used — stole something that belonged to them." She took an audible breath and exhaled slowly.

"So the question is. . ." She met Stephanie's concerned gaze then. "I mean, I know you don't feel I'm — ruined for you, for God's sake. I would know if you felt that way. But do you feel at all like something has been taken from you?" She continued to study Stephanie's face until Stephanie looked away again.

Frowning, Stephanie crushed her cigarette on the step, then picked up the filter and dropped it into the empty cup. "I don't see you as my possession."

"No," Marian said gently, "I know that. But I also know that part of my anger has been what might be considered," she smiled wryly, "politically incorrect."

Stephanie chuckled in response. "I'm not sure either of us would get any awards for being politically correct, even on our best days."

Marian laughed softly. She put her arm around Stephanie's waist, and Stephanie pulled her close.

"It's hard to admit this," Marian whispered, and a tinge of pink colored her cheeks.

Stephanie gave Marian a one-armed sympathetic hug.

Marian closed her eyes and leaned against Stephanie. "When I made my commitment to our relationship, I did it fully, completely. Nothing held back." She paused. "I gave you my heart."

Stephanie tightened her hold, and Marian smiled with the embrace. She opened her eyes and looked at their joined hands resting on Stephanie's thigh.

"Well, one day not long after we began living together, I realized that I had given you something else. Something I thought I would never give anyone. I knew that first night that I was trusting you with a part of me that I had never trusted to anyone else. But what I didn't know for a while was just how total that — surrender had been. I was in class that day. My students were finishing a final exam, and I had started grading some of the papers that had already been turned in. I don't know why it happened just then, but I found myself thinking about you. It was as though you had walked up behind me and put your arms around me." She smiled. "It was a little like that night in Karen's library. It seemed as if we were in bed. I felt naked, and I could feel your hands on me, caressing me, making love to me." She made a small, contented sound. "The next thing I knew, a student was talking to me, and I pulled out of it somehow. Later, I wondered if you were thinking about me and maybe you had done it intentionally, even knowing where I was." She patted Stephanie's hand reassuringly. "Remember, I hadn't known you very well then. I know now you wouldn't have done it deliberately."

Stephanie smiled. "I suppose it would have been a natural assumption at the time. After all, that night in Karen's library, you hadn't exactly invited me to intrude on you like that."

"No, but I really couldn't blame you for that," Marian said. "You were naturally so overwhelmed by my obvious physical charms. You simply couldn't help yourself."

Stephanie laughed, and Marian raised an eyebrow. She poked Stephanie in the ribs with a mock-threatening finger. "Are you going to sit there and tell me that is not true?"

Chuckling, Stephanie shook her head and grabbed Marian's hand. "No. I must confess that when I saw you, the first thing that struck me were your very obvious physical charms." She took a deep breath and looked at Marian tenderly. "And then when you looked at me, I felt as if I might fall into those incredible eyes of yours and never come out again."

Marian's eyes melted. "Well, you have definitely saved yourself," she whispered. She cleared her throat. "Anyway, following closely on the heels of the thought that you might be intentionally toying with my mind that day was the thought that — I didn't *care* if you had done it intentionally or not." Her words became slow, measured. "That I had somehow given you the *right* to do that. The right to touch me in any way you wanted — whenever you wanted. I had never felt that way about anyone before. And I knew I never would."

She took a deep breath and let it out before she continued. "I *wanted* you to possess me. I wanted to belong to you in some way that I don't know how to explain. It was quite a revelation." She caressed Stephanie's hand, her voice a whisper. "It was as if I had presented you with a gift. The biggest gift I had ever given to anyone — could ever give to anyone in my life." She raised their entwined hands and kissed the back of Stephanie's hand then held it to her cheek for a moment, her eyes closed. "I needed to say that now. Before, I've only said it in bed, where it was safe. Where it might seem that I meant it as just a sexual game." She lowered their hands to Stephanie's thigh again. "But it goes deeper than that, my love."

Marian looked up. Stephanie's eyes were closed, and when she opened them, a tear trickled down her cheek. Marian gently wiped it away with her fingertips. When Stephanie spoke, her words were strangled.

"And when he raped you, you felt as if he had taken that gift from me — a gift you had given with so much love." Tears coursed down her cheeks, but she seemed unaware of them. "I know," she whispered. "It was one of the reasons I wanted to kill him." She turned and took Marian's face in her hands. Her gaze was tender, her love pouring out in waves. "I want you to know," she said with soft intensity, "that he can never take that from us. That gift is a treasure I keep deep inside of me. It's safe there, and it always will be." She searched Marian's eyes. "I have always known about that gift — and how much it meant to you. And it has meant even more to me."

Weeping, Marian nodded, closed her eyes, and put her head on Stephanie's shoulder. She sighed deeply, as if a weight had been lifted. They held one another for a time, and then Marian smiled shakily. "Kleenex time," she whispered.

When she came back, she was blowing her nose and carrying a box of tissues. She extended them to Stephanie, who pulled out a couple and wiped her eyes. They looked at each other and laughed.

"We're a fine pair, huh?" Marian giggled.

"Definitely." Stephanie grinned.

"Back to business?"

Stephanie nodded and patted the step beside her.

Marian sat and was silent for a moment, then she said, "Would you ever feel resentful of it, Stef? I mean, if we decide to have it, would you ever feel it was taking my love from you?"

"You have enough love for more than one person. Sometimes I think you have more love in you than anyone I've ever known."

"You're sweet," Marian said softly and leaned over to kiss Stephanie's earlobe. Stephanie smiled and squeezed Marian's thigh.

"Well," Marian said, "I guess if you ever felt neglected, I'd just have to take the time to give you a little more attention, wouldn't I?"

Stephanie chuckled at Marian's tone. "You're insatiable," she said, shaking her head.

Marian lifted an eyebrow. "Complaining?"

Stephanie laughed and said with exaggerated quickness, "No. No, ma'am. No, I am not."

"Saved twice in one day," Marian smiled, then she sighed heavily and frowned. "You know, there's also how the child would feel — knowing its father. . ." She paused. "Damn. I hate to keep calling it an 'it,' but I guess that's what it is right now."

"If the child is born, it will be a boy," Stephanie said quietly.

Marian closed her eyes and groaned. "God. That would be even worse. At least if it were a girl, the resemblance might be less likely."

"No. Any feeling you would have like that would disappear very quickly."

"I don't know," Marian grimaced. "So, anyway, how would *he* feel, knowing what had happened?" She groaned again. "And what about the fact that his mother and her lover are lesbians? We still don't have the Good Housekeeping Seal of Approval for *that* one."

Stephanie lit another cigarette. "Children can deal with almost anything if they have enough love. Or at least, they can work it out for themselves more easily if they know they're loved." She smiled. "I believe I've heard you say that."

Marian nodded and then frowned. "Of course, there's also how having a child would affect our lives. We've been so independent. That would certainly change." She made an exasperated sound. "There are so many damned things against it, Stef!"

Stephanie nodded and studied the tip of her cigarette. "How much longer can you wait to decide?"

"It would be best not to wait past the second month. There are more risks after that."

Stephanie squeezed Marian's hand firmly. "By then, you'll know what's best to do. It will be very clear to you by then."

Marian met Stephanie's eyes. "And you, sweetheart? Will you know for sure by then?"

"Yes," Stephanie said quietly, "I'll know, too."

1

Frank Talbot cut the engine on the motorboat near the mouth of the inlet and allowed it to drift. After a minute or so, he picked up the stout pole next to his feet and pushed the craft closer to the shore that sloped up on his right.

The racket of crickets rose and fell as he reached out and grabbed at a wet root that poked out of the black water. Leaning over the side, he looped the tie-rope around the root and then settled back on the seat again. His eyes had grown accustomed to the dark of the inlet, and now he could make out vague shapes in the back-yards of the houses that sat on top of the rise past the tangled live-oak woods. From where the boat was, two other houses sat between him and his target.

The moon had risen a long time ago — minutes after the fisher-man with the boat had gurgled away his life almost two miles away, his body stuffed among the roots of trees like the ones Talbot stared past now. He looked up at the cold-white, malevolent eye that glared down at him, and he felt uneasy. He had awakened in the brush alongside the road before the moon had been washed out by the sun this morning, his skin crawling from the old nightmare — the eyes closing in on him, pinning him to the ground, squeezing his chest until he could barely breathe.

A chill creeped between his shoulder blades, and he shuddered and closed his eyes.

She was doing this to him.

But soon, the nightmares would disappear. Forever.

The closest house topping the rise past the woods glowed with lights in back. The next house was dark. There was a light over the back door of the bitch's house, but as he watched, the light winked out. He flipped back the cover on the luminous-dial watch. Eleven-thirty.

He waited patiently. The dark water slapped against the sides of the boat, pushed it out and then back to scrape softly against the roots. Finally, the lights went off in the first house. Twelve-fifteen.

He pulled the boat closer to the bank, hauled his leg over the side and stepped out, slipping on the wet roots. He climbed the gentle rise of ground, hugging the earth in a crouching position. As he reached the middle of the woods, he dropped to his belly and began to crawl.

Just like Nam, he grinned in the blackness of the trees that hid him from the moon.

2

"Hon, you want some hot tea before bed?" Marian called out from the kitchen, where she was folding the dishtowel over the rack.

It had been a long day. Time and again, they had come back to the question that was lying on their minds with such heaviness.

The child that was growing inside of her.

She sighed. Their lives would be so different if she decided to have the child. And, although she wanted them both to make the decision, ultimately it would be hers. Stephanie would not push her one way or the other, but would support her in whatever she decided. And it would be heartfelt support, Marian knew, not just lip service. She felt a chill, and she shuddered with the suddenness of it.

Assuming they were alive. Assuming the father of the child did not kill the mother.

She turned and began running water into the tea kettle, then stopped. Stephanie apparently had not heard her. She called again, but when there was still no answer, she put the kettle down and went to the living room door.

"Stef?"

Stephanie sat on the sofa, her hands resting on her thighs, her head held at the familiar cocked angle, as if she were listening intently to some distant voice. Her eyes were open, staring vacantly, and her body seemed stiff.

"Stephanie," Marian said softly and approached her. Still no response. She laid her hand on Stephanie's shoulder.

Stephanie's eyes closed, and a tremor passed through her body. Finally, she opened her eyes and met Marian's worried look. She took a long, deep breath and let it out slowly. "He's coming," she whisered, as if her mouth were dry.

Marian felt her stomach drop and heard a small, involuntary sound escape from her throat.

Stephanie reached over to the coffee table and picked up the communication device that linked them to the police officers in the car two blocks away. The oblong black box squealed briefly, then a male voice said, "We're here, Ms. Nowland."

"I feel him very close now," Stephanie said.

There was a moment of silence before the voice replied, "Thanks for the warning. We'll be watching closely. The first sound you hear, let us know."

Stephanie pushed the disconnect button. "There's really nothing more they can do." She looked at Marian. "If they move now, we'll be back where we started."

"Do you think we ought to call Gary?"

"I'm afraid he'd rush over. Maybe we should wait a while."

Marian smiled shakily. "You're right, of course. I guess I'm just getting cold feet at the last minute."

Stephanie rubbed at the frown lines in her forehead for a minute, then she reached for the telephone. "Let's call it off. I don't want to put you through this. We'll find another way."

But as her hand lifted the receiver, Marian stopped her. "No," she said quietly, her voice steady now. "It's our only chance of having it over. We decided this after we looked at all the other options, and nothing's changed." She took the receiver from Stephanie and placed it in the cradle. "I want this over."

"Well, this is the dregs, ain't it?" Detective James Hobart sighed heavily and made a clicking noise with his upper dental plate against his lower teeth. He lifted both hands to the steering wheel and pushed against it.

Detective Steve Michaels slumped further in the seat of the unmarked car and rubbed his eyes. "Yeah," he said, yawning. "Yeah, it is."

Hobart glanced at his partner. He looked ghostly in the glow of the streetlight half a block away. "You tired, kid?"

"A little." A long time ago, Michaels had given up trying to change Hobart's view of him as a kid who was wet behind the ears.

"Been getting too much, huh?" Hobart grinned in the semi-darkness.

"As a matter of fact, Hobie," Michaels said in mild exasperation, "I didn't get much sleep last night because Gracie's daughter has been staying with us while her dad is out of town, and she got sick. We were up with her until four in the morning."

Hobart sucked at his teeth and grinned again. "Yeah, but you get plenty from that new little wife of yours, don't you, kid? Marrying a woman who's had a husband before — especially if she's been without for a while — always makes her a little more eager in the sack."

Michaels turned and stared at Hobart. "Is that all you've got on your mind?"

Hobart shrugged. "Sex is a fact of life, boy. We all need it."

Michaels turned back and shook his head in disgust.

Five minutes passed in silence. Hobart fidgeted. He had turned fifty-two back in the spring, and it seemed as if he had less patience now than when he was younger. Maybe it was knowing he didn't have so much time left any more. Or, more likely, he considered, it was the way his hemorrhoids were acting up again. "You know," he said, "this whole thing's a crock."

"What is?"

"Well, we been sitting out here every night till two in the morning for nothing. And then Baker and Turner come on, and *they* sit here for nothing. All because Achison believes this Nowland broad can see the future." He spat out the window.

"I don't know, Hobie. She's supposed to be pretty good at what she does. Gracie told me she saw her name in the papers — five, maybe six years ago — when all those old ladies were being killed up in Jacksonville. She fingered the man. And Gracie's got a friend who — well, I don't know, consults her or something every once in a while."

Hobart spat again, more a gesture of disbelief and derision than from necessity. "A crock. Something funny in Jax. There was a tip or something. Can't nobody tell the future or see things like that."

Michaels sighed and decided not to argue. It wouldn't do any good, anyway.

"If you ask me," Hobart continued, "Achison's just got us out here to make himself look good to that dame. The young one."

"What?"

"I was with him the other night when we were setting it up. Her and her girlfriend. He's hot for the girlfriend."

"Come on, Hobie. Get off it, will you?"

"No." Hobart shook his head emphatically. "I'm serious. I saw the way he looked at her. His wife left him, and he's looking for another piece of action." He chuckled. "Or a piece of something." He clicked his teeth. "Tell you the truth, I was taking her in, too. She's a good-looking broad." He motioned with his hands at his chest. "Tits out to here."

"Oh, Jesus Christ."

Hobart chuckled again. He was used to the kid's reaction to his observations, and sometimes he made stronger observations just to get the reaction.

There was a squawk of static, and Michaels thumbed the button on the black box on the seat.

"We're here, Ms. Nowland."

"I feel him very close now."

Michaels frowned and felt a flutter in his stomach at the tone of the woman's voice. "Thanks for the warning. We'll be watching closely. The first sound you hear, let us know." He released the button and glanced at Hobart.

Hobart shook his head and then tapped his temple with his forefinger. "A crock."

After several minutes of silence, Hobart drummed his fingertips
on the steering wheel and turned to look at Michaels. "You know
they're queer, don't you?"

"What?" It was a tired sound, filled with resignation.

"Queers, lezzies." Hobart grinned. "Cunt-lappers, Stevie boy."
He ignored Michaels' cool silence. "Of course, the older one — the
fortuneteller—"

"She's not a fortuneteller, Hobart. She's a professional psychic.
There's a difference."

"Whatever. She ain't bad-looking either, but you can tell she's a
dyke. More so'n the other one."

Michaels' voice became chillier. "How can you tell, Hobie? Was
she wearing a sign?"

Hobart shot him a glance and clicked his teeth again. "Short
hair, way she walks," he said authoritatively.

"For Christ's sake, Hobie, Gracie's got short hair, too. And she's
athletic."

"That's different."

"Why's that different?"

Hobart looked at him condescendingly. "'Cause Gracie ain't a
dyke."

Michaels stared across the darkness. "That makes no sense,
Hobie. No sense at all."

Hobart shrugged and looked at his watch. "Shit. One o'clock.
Well, only another hour, and Baker'll be here. I'm gonna stretch a
little."

"Is that a good idea? She says he's close now. We'll be more
noticeable, and we don't want to scare him off."

Hobart looked at Michaels and then got out of the car. Standing, he bent and slapped his hand on the open window rest. "You
still think something's going to happen, don't you, kid?" He grinned.
"I tell you, ain't nobody after them. Just call in the hourly check,
okay?"

Michaels sighed, reached for the radio, and waved Hobart
away. He reported in and slumped down in the seat again. If anything happened at the house, they wouldn't be able to see it; they

were parked too far away. The women would call them back. And Hobart would see anything coming up from their side.

4

Talbot wiped the back of his hand across his mouth and frowned, studying the lines that slithered through the wall of the house near its gable.

It seemed too easy. Something was wrong. The back of his neck tingled, and his hands were cold and clammy.

He sank to his stomach again and angled toward the backyard of the house next door.

5

Hobart hitched up his pants and lit another cigarette. He puffed at it, then walked a few yards further away from the car. Something rattled in the bushes, and he whirled. His eyes narrowed, and he stood still. As a squirrel darted from the ground and shot up a tree nearby, he hitched up his pants again and grinned. Getting jumpy in his old age.

As he turned back, a hand caught at the back of his head. The razor-like blade whispered across his throat. His knees buckled, and he slumped to the ground, his mouth opening spastically to call out a warning to the kid. But the only sound he could make was a gurgle as his blood pumped from the mouth that had been opened across his throat.

Michaels shifted in the seat, looked at his watch, and closed his eyes again. No matter how tired he was when he got home, he'd get into a hot shower and . . . He heard a rustle in the bushes to the rear of the car and jerked himself upright. He started to turn to find Hobart. The knife did not give him time to complete the movement.

Stephanie dropped the cup of tea on the floor, shattering the cup. The dark, hot liquid spread across the linoleum.

Marian jumped, and a small cry escaped from her.

"I think they're dead," Stephanie whispered.

Gary flung his jacket into the vinyl armchair and draped his tie over it. He sat down heavily and rubbed at his eyes.

It had been another dead end in the killing at the convenience store holdup this morning. People just didn't pay attention. But it was understandable, he knew. He had seen it time and again. When somebody's holding a gun on you, you don't notice what color his hair or eyes are, what he's wearing. A dozen people could be there, and you'd get a dozen different descriptions. You see the gun. That's all. The ugly bore of the gun staring you in the face.

He got up and crossed the room to the built-in kitchen in the small efficiency apartment. The refrigerator beside the sink was tiny, but it scarcely made any difference because he rarely kept anything in it. Ever since he had moved out of the house, he seemed to eat most of his meals out anyway. He took out a package of bologna, smelled it, and decided it was good for at least one more day. But the bread was moldy. He leaned against the sink and sighed.

Jenny had been right. He had taken her for granted so many times. He'd get home at night, pull off his shoes, use her for a sounding board for his problems, eat the dinner she had prepared for him, and then, more often than not, fall asleep in front of the television. When she protested that she needed something more in her life, he had patted her rump and laughed patronizingly at the problems he thought were "all in her head." Take a few night classes, he had said; get involved in the wives' bridge group. After all, his mother had always been at home, had never seemed to need anything outside of her husband and children.

"Bastard," he muttered to himself. "Goddamned, insensitive,

stupid bastard." Jenny wasn't his mother. But it was only when she was gone that he realized what he needed was a partner.

If they could be together now, it would be different. He would make sure it was different. It wouldn't come easy to him, but he was willing to work on it. He sighed. It was doubtful that he would have the chance.

Now, Jenny was finally doing what she wanted to do apart from him and his childish demands. She was going back to school, preparing herself for a more independent life. And she was dating other men. Maybe sleeping with other men. He clenched his fists. He felt his eyes burn, and he rubbed at them again with the heels of his hands.

In so many ways, Marian reminded him of Jenny. That independence he had finally been able to see in Jenny just before they separated. And the sensuousness that he had taken for granted until she was no longer in his bed every night. In a way, it was probably that spark in Marian that had caused him to look at his relationship with Jenny in a different light — see how he might have caused her to leave him, instead of putting all the blame on her. It had been a harsh awakening.

He had begun to question why Marian, who seemed so much like Jenny, had stayed with someone all those years while Jenny had left him. Early on, he had dismissed the notion that it had anything to do with the fact that Marian and Stephanie were women. It was a human question, not an issue of sexual preference.

And slowly, as the days had passed, as he watched Marian and Stephanie together, he had begun to detect the difference. Marian, like Jenny, he thought, needed to be a person in her own right. Apart from being his wife. He had never seen that before. It was something he had chosen to ignore. It was something Marian had with Stephanie that Jenny had not been able to have with him.

When he had seen Jenny last week, he had tried to explain to her what he had learned while she had been gone. But she was still hesitant. And he couldn't blame her. How was she to know that he had really begun to see things differently?

He threw the bread into the trash can and after only a second's hesitation, sent the bologna after it.

It would take time, he thought. But maybe some day she would believe that he was willing to change. *Had* changed.

He got a bottle of Coke from the refrigerator and went to sit on the sofa again. Cradling the receiver on his shoulder, he popped off the cap and considered calling her. He looked at his watch. 1:05. He smiled wryly. Calling her at one in the morning certainly wouldn't win him any points. He put the bottle to his lips and dropped the receiver back with the other hand. The fact that it did not rest squarely on the disconnect buttons passed his notice. He set the bottle down and headed for the bathroom to take a shower.

It was forty-five seconds before the telephone began blasting its alert that the receiver was off the hook. By that time, he had the shower going and the bathroom door closed. By the time he stepped out of the steamy shower, the signal had switched itself off. He lay down on the sofa, just for a short nap, he told himself, before checking on the stakeout.

8

Talbot lay at the back corner of the house and mapped out his next move.

The telephone lines first, he thought. Then the alarm system. The alarm system could be tricky. And after that, he'd jimmy the back door and be home free. He took a deep breath and exhaled slowly, trying to restore the calm he had felt in the boat. First things first. All he had to do was get across the backyard to the telephone lines. He had time. Plenty of time.

He lay there, listening for noises inside the house. The lights had been out when he had gotten back from the two cops. That was going to make it easier. He rose to a crouching position and started his short run through the dangerous moonlight to the other side of the house.

Halfway there, his peripheral vision caught something that was so unexpected, so mind-jolting, that he jerked his head toward it, failed to see a tree root jutting out of the earth, slipped, and lost his footing. He fell heavily, just breaking his fall by throwing his hands out in front of him. The knife scooted a few feet out of his reach, and he scrabbled for it in the moonlight that pooled around him. As he stood, slightly shaken from the fall, he stared at the house.

His palms were suddenly wet with sweat. He wiped his left hand on his pants, shifted the knife to his left hand, wiped his right hand, then shifted the knife back again.

This wasn't the way it was supposed to be. He licked at lips that had grown dry. He was supposed to have cut the phone lines, disengaged the alarm system, jimmied the door, then . . . He shook his head, trying to clear the confusion. It made no sense.

The door was open.

He stood there, paralyzed, with that one thought careening through his mind.

The door was open!

He felt sweat trickle down his side from his armpit. He rubbed at his jaw with the knuckles of the hand that held the knife and felt something sticky. He looked down. Blood had run down the blade onto the handle and onto the back of his hand. When his hands had begun to sweat, the dried blood had gotten sticky again. He wiped his hand on his pants once more.

Finally, he felt as if his mind were beginning to clear. His breathing became more regular, his heart seemed to be settling back down in his chest. He found he could think.

His eyes narrowed slightly. There must be a cop in there with them. Maybe a lot of cops. The minute he put one foot in there, they'd jump him and blow him away. They'd splash his brains all over the walls the minute he walked in. He started to shake slightly. Then he remembered. There couldn't be any cops. He had looked, hadn't he? Hadn't he heard what the two down the block said? He had waited long enough at the side to know there was nobody else in there.

They were alone. They had to be.

And it would be a while before the cops who were on the street were due to call in again.

It wasn't the way he wanted it. He wanted time to play with them. Time to make them suffer for what the bitch had done to him. And now he didn't have that time.

He stood and watched the pool of moonlight in the doorway. And he suddenly felt the urge to run. To turn and run down the bank and get into the boat and leave.

But if he did that, he would have to wait a long time before he came back.

He was going to kill her.

And it had to be now.

Now.

It had to be now. Kill them and then get away clean.

He stared at the open door.

They were waiting for him. The way the gooks had waited for him in the village in Nam.

What were they doing in there?

Then a smile started to spread across his hard mouth.

They were only women. Like that little gook in Nam. And she hadn't given him too hard a time.

And besides, the young one. She had to be afraid of him. That would work in his favor, too.

He could take care of both of them.

Now.

He slowly climbed the three steps leading to the door. Then he waited. Take your time, he told himself. Take your time. You've got the time.

He reached out and pushed gently at the door so that it rested against the wall in back of it. Reaching inside on the left for the light switch he remembered from the time he was there before, he held it firmly between his thumb and forefinger and noislessly pushed it up instead of letting it click into place. Nothing. Once, twice more, he pushed the switch up and down. Still nothing. He frowned.

But he was beginning to feel his hands grow steadier with each move.

He waited until his eyes adjusted to the darkened room. The moonlight was dim, but after a while, he could see shadows in the room. He stepped in fully. The door to the living room was closed. To his right, the door into the hall was open.

Softly, he crossed the room, step by step, slowly, alert for any noise. He felt as if his ears were straining in the dark.

In the hall was probably where the fuse box was. The light out in the kitchen had given him an idea. Just pull all the fuses, he grinned; then he'd be in control.

At the door to the hall, he stopped and ran over in his mind the layout of the house.

When he stepped through the door, a small alcove would be to his right; that was the most likely place for the fuse box. Straight in front of him would be the hall. On the right of the hall, the first door opened onto the bathroom. A bit further down, the second door opened onto the bedroom, and at the end of the hall, the third door opened onto the same bedroom. On the left, at the end of the hall, there was only one door. It led to the room where he had found the young one's papers and other things. And there was a door that connected the two rooms inside, and a door that left from the bitch's office into the living room.

He frowned. Every room in the house had two doors. He could come in one, and they'd go out the other.

He smiled. It would make it harder, and maybe that would be more fun. The house was like a maze. It had the mice, and it had the cat now. Cat and mouse.

And he was the cat.

The mice were just waiting. Waiting for the cops to come and release them from the trap.

But a sudden thought pricked at the back of his neck again.

Why was the door open?

He frowned again and rubbed at his mouth. Then he almost giggled at the next thought.

Because they thought he was the mouse.

He stifled a laugh. They would find out different.

They wanted him further into the house. So that's where *they* were. They were hiding in there, thinking they only had to keep him there for a little while, until the cops from the street showed up. He stepped through the hall doorway and flattened himself against the wall. He listened. Nothing.

He moved into the alcove to the right and felt along the wall. The fuse box opened easily, quietly, and he ran his fingers over the inside. All the fuses were missing. He gritted his teeth, and his jaw muscles worked almost painfully.

They couldn't have done it that fast, he knew. Most of the fuses must have been taken out before he even showed up. Which meant they had been planning to be inside the house.

He felt something strange at the edge of his mind. As if a cold finger had been laid against his temple. He frowned and shook his head and felt the sweat trickle down his side. He felt chilled. His heart was pounding again.

But he had to get them now, his mind screamed at him.

Now.

Slowly, he made his way from the fuse box back toward the hallway. But just as he was almost into the hall, the finger against his temple became an icy hand that felt as if it were scrabbling at the back of his neck. He stifled a scream and crouched in the alcove, shaking, his eyes straining with fear, sweat dripping into them.

It was in this fog of fear that he heard, as if from a very long distance, the back door close, the bolt-lock click into place, and the key grate as it was removed from the lock. His head jerked spastically toward the sound, and his clenched hands came up to cover his ears.

In the bedroom, Stephanie doubled over from the sudden nausea that threatened to overwhelm her. She clenched her fists and pressed them into her eyes. She heard the lock click and knew Marian was still in the kitchen. She had to hold onto him for just another minute. *Just another minute.* Just long enough for Marian to get back into the living room.

She had known it would be bad, she thought, had known it would be terribly hard. But this, this was worse than she had believed it could be. The instant she had opened her mind to his, she had felt this agonizing pain and nausea flood her body, as if a tidal wave were looming over her and then crashing down with sickening force, smothering her.

She straightened slightly and put her fists at her sides.

Concentration. She had to maintain the concentration. She made herself stand up fully and take long deep breaths to calm her lurching stomach.

She heard the living room door squeak. It was so soft, she wasn't sure whether she had heard it or merely sensed it. But there should have been time. She relaxed slightly and withdrew from Talbot's mind to give herself time to gather her strength again. The nausea faded, and her breathing grew calmer, more regular.

She knew now that she would not be able to maintain constant control over his mind. She was going to have to conserve her strength for the times she needed it most.

Talbot tried to stand and felt his knees start to buckle, as if they were made of water. He took a deep breath and stood slowly, supporting himself against the wall as he rose. He shook his head and rubbed at the back of his neck with his free hand. He leaned against the wall and waited until he felt steadier. Until the fear subsided.

The bitch. She was doing it to him. He had never felt fear before, he raged. *Never*, he screamed silently. *Never*.

She was putting it into his mind.

And for that, he would put the knife at her heart and rip it out slowly. Very slowly.

He calmed the rage as quickly as he could. Put it simmering on the burner so he could think clearly once more.

He began moving up the hall, his back sliding against the wall. He held the knife low, his hand clenched on it hard, slightly in front of him. His other hand was held out, as if fending off an imaginary enemy.

Across the door from the bathroom, he paused again, listening for anything that would give them away. Nothing. He looked at the bathroom door and dragged his arm across his sweating face. He looked back toward the door into the kitchen. He knew one of them had disappeared into the living room after locking the door. Their plan must be to lure him into the other rooms, since he couldn't get out the back door, and the front door would be too dangerous to use. Then, when they had him far enough into the house, they could use the key to get out the back door and escape if the cops hadn't come by then.

He shook his head. Why wouldn't they just use the front door and get away?

Did they really think they could outwit him at a game he could play so well? He almost laughed.

They thought they were cats. They would learn that they were mice in *his* trap. He grinned in the darkness. The trap they had made for themselves.

Moving slowly, silently, he went back to the swinging door that led from the kitchen into the hall, reached down and picked up the wooden wedge that held the door open, took the few steps from that door to the door that led to the living room, and wedged the wood into place. Now, when they thought they had trapped him and wanted to make their exit out the back door, he would have them exactly where he wanted them: In the living room, where he would block the front door, and this little piece of wood would block the back. He smiled and stifled a chuckle.

Then he turned and made his way back down the hall. At the bathroom door, he stepped inside, and his hand sought the key on the other side of the door. He closed the door, locked it from the outside, and dropped the key into his shirt pocket. It would never do to leave any hiding place for his mice. ·

Reaching the door of the bedroom, he stood for a few seconds, listening. Then he reached for the doorknob. He turned it carefully, slowly. It turned easily in his hand.

Pushing the door gently with his foot, he flattened himself against the doorjamb and stared into the room. The curtains at the window on the opposite side of the room were parted slightly, allowing a thin finger of moonlight to enter the darkness. It lay across the bed and touched the dresser on his side of the room. And it lightened the room enough so he could see with a fair amount of clearness after the darkness of the hall.

But the dresser between the two doors cut off his view of the bottom half of the other door. In order to find out if one of his mice were hiding there, he was going to have to move into the middle of the room. Softly, he closed the door he was standing next to, turned the key in the lock, and pocketed it. Crouching, he moved to the corner of the dresser, the knife held in front of him. But as he stood slightly to round the corner, the fear chilled the back of his neck again.

Without warning, the eyes were all around him, mocking him, staring at him. He whimpered as he saw eyes floating in on the moonlight, and then he was stepping on them, squishing them under his feet. He pushed his knuckles against his mouth and fought back the moan and closed his eyes tightly, pleading for the staring, drifting eyes to go away. When he saw the door on the other side of the dresser open, he could do nothing about it.

Stephanie pressed herself against the door inside Marian's office and swallowed the sour bile back into her throat. She was trembling violently, and for the first time, she was unsure whether she could continue to enter his mind at will. This time, she had had to delve further into his subconcious to trigger the fear. And she knew that he was aware now of what was happening to him, and that awareness was enabling him to push her away more quickly. Each time, she would have to use more and more force to accomplish less and less. Soon, he would be able to hold her off when she began the push, and he would be battling back at her.

Already, she could hear the bedroom door being locked, then she heard the floorboard creak as he began to move across the hall to the other side of the door she was leaning against.

Cat and mouse. Cat and mouse.

She couldn't get the words out of her head.

She hadn't counted on his locking the doors behind him as he went through the house looking for them. At this point, of course, they could escape at any time. But then, that wasn't the point of this whole macabre game. The point was to keep him here until he could be captured and sent out of their lives. All they could do was play the game for the time it would take for the police to realize they were alone.

Her gut-wrenching feeling was that they would be too late.

As silently as she could, she moved across the room to the door that connected Marian's office to hers. The thought occurred to her to lock the door behind her, but if she did that, he would simply go back down the hall to the living room.

And that's where Marian was.

9

At the Saint Augustine police station, the officer on the desk drummed his fingers on the counter. Hobart and Michaels were too late with their last call. Baker and Turner were due to report to the stakeout in fifteen minutes. He glanced at the wall clock.

It was too long to wait, he decided.

10

Police officer Valerie Thomas sipped at the steaming coffee in the Dunkin' Donuts shop on San Marcos Avenue and waited for her partner, Earl Kominsky, to emerge from the men's room. She smiled slightly. It had taken two months for her to get the message across without scaring him. She had almost made a mistake at first, coming on too strongly. After all, her aggressiveness had gotten her a place on the police force, and it was hard to shift gears to accommodate Earl's innate shyness with women.

But finally. She smiled again. An innocent cup of coffee at her apartment after their shift. She had changed into "something more comfortable," and then, while she stood over the perking coffee, he apparently had gotten up his courage. When she turned, she found herself in his arms.

And she had melted. Just melted. She stared into the coffee dreamily for a minute and then laughed at herself. She was acting like a schoolgirl with her first crush, and she was twenty-five years old. Silly. But he had been so gentle with her, so tender. She sipped at the coffee. And surprisingly passionate and forceful, too. That last time, he had taken her so slowly, so exquisitely slowly, that she had thought she would scream. *Damn*, she remembered with a smile, she *had* screamed. There were a lot of things she liked about Earl. It was good to know that their compatibility extended to the bedroom.

Now, Earl emerged from the back of the restaurant and walked towards her, his thumbs hooked in his belt. He grinned as he saw her looking at him, and a blush spread across his broad face. He threw a leg over the stool and sat down.

"Don't look now," she said with a soft laugh, "but I think you're swaggering."

He rubbed the back of his neck, and the blush deepened. "Sorry. I don't mean to act like that, but I guess I'm feeling pretty full of myself."

Valerie took a bite of the still-warm, sugary doughnut. After a minute, she looked at him. "It's okay. You've got a right to swagger a little, I guess. I don't think I've ever been bedded quite so thoroughly — or enjoyed it so much."

Earl blushed furiously and opened his mouth, but the squawk-box on his shoulder strap staticked into life. They listened intently, their eyes locked for a minute, and then they were up and running for the door, Earl flinging a bill on the counter as they ran out to the car.

They were crossing King Street, just past the Bridge of Lions, when a drunk driver came barreling into the intersection and caught the patrol car broadside on Valerie's side. Her head was slammed against the window, and unconsciousness was thrown over her like a warm blanket.

Earl managed to get his car door open, but a sword of glass from the windshield had pierced his arm, severing the artery across the inside of his elbow. Blood spurted into the street as he pulled himself from the car and sat down on the curb, his back to the Plaza.

He tried to remember what he was doing when the accident occurred, but he was finding it hard to concentrate. He stared at Valerie in the car, her head resting against the window. *Have to get Valerie out of the car*, he thought, but there seemed to be a fog settling over everything. He stood up, rubbed at his temples, and when he saw the blood running more freely, he attemped to press the wound with his other hand. The blood ran between his fingers and dripped into the gutter.

The drunk sat down on the curb and cried and told Earl how sorry he was.

11

At the police station, the officer on duty tried again to reach Detective Sergeant Gary Achison. The line was still busy. He disconnected, frowned, and dialed the operator.

12

In her office, Stephanie pressed herself against the wall beside the huge dieffenbachia that stood to the hinged side of the door. Light filtered in through the lightweight drapes from the streetlight closest to the house. She fought an insane urge to laugh. If they had known a killer would have been coming after them, they would have bought heavier drapes.

She bit at her lip, pressed her eyelids tightly together, and stifled a cry that threatened to break from her. Her heart pounded in her chest so loudly she was sure he would be able to hear it. She felt his presence on the other side of the door, and her throat ached with the need to scream.

Then, the knob was turning. Slow, slow.

Concentration.

She needed the concentration again. She took a long, deep breath as silently as she could and released it just as silently. She had to stop him here. Here, before he could get to Marian again.

The door began to swing open as if in slow-motion, an inch at a time. The top hinge squealed suddenly, and the door stopped. After a long minute, it began opening again, until it rested against the planter. She could see the door being pushed against the planter, saw it give slightly, then the door stopped again.

She felt his thoughts, although she had not entered his mind. The questioning. What was on the other side of the door? Another slight push and the realization that there was a stationary object behind it.

Stephanie looked down and saw the tip of the shoe protrude past the door. It stayed there for what seemed to be an eternity.

There was a shoe in the door.

A shoe.

She shook her head to shake loose the persistent thought. In an effort to regain control, she pulled the psychic curtain tightly around her consciousness. She had to give him time to enter the room fully, then attack him, lock the door he had entered from, leave the room, and lock that one behind her. Perhaps the time he spent trying to open the doors again would give the police time to get there. In his all-consuming need to kill them, he would not even consider leaving through the window.

She watched as he stepped into the room, the knife held in front of him and his other hand held in front and to the side, as if he were readying himself for an attack. He took another cautious step, then he was turning slowly toward her. She heard his breathing — slow, regular, as if he were consciously directing it the way she was controlling her own.

As his head turned, he finally saw her, and she felt the sudden dread again that she would not be able to stop him. His lips curled into a soundless laugh that chilled her. The black curly hair glinted for a second in the streetlight glow. He turned fully to face her and took a sideways step to keep her in his view.

He was almost far enough into the room, she thought. Just another step. Just one more step.

And as she saw him take that step, she pushed the curtain away and shot out the mental, ghostly fingers to touch his mind.

It was as if she had entered a fetid, steaming jungle. The overgrowth tangled around her, an odor of mold and decay rose around her in nauseating waves. There were no rooms here, no well-ordered rooms, neat hallways that opened onto memories of the past that had been locked away and could be looked into with some semblance of sanity.

Here, there were roots that snaked up to claw at her ankles, monstrous tropical vegetation that dangled over her head and wrapped themselves around her throat, choking her, smothering her.

The eyes she had seen before and used against him.

She saw him roll off the body of a dead Vietnamese woman and crouch in horror as a young man entered the hut, stared at the scene before him, and left.

Stephanie squeezed that memory hard. It seemed to be the one that held the most terror for him. And as she pressed against that terror, the man in the room in front of her began to breathe asthmatically, wheezing in fearful gasps as if he could not catch his breath.

But just as she saw him stagger backwards, the overpowering nausea at the violence and smell of the blood from twenty years ago overwhelmed her, and she slumped against the wall, her stomach threatening to empty itself.

Talbot staggered back and grasped onto the edge of the desk to support himself. As Stephanie tried to regain control, his mind pushed back at her, and she felt the rage and hatred crash over her. The blackness crept closer, and she fought it for as long as she could, but it finally fell as a fog across her consciousness, and she felt her knees crumple just before she hit the floor. As she fell, a stab of pain shot through her right knee, and it was only that brief pain that kept her from succumbing completely to the blackness that threatened to engulf her.

She saw him through the fog, a terrifying shadow that slithered toward her, a low, gurgling, triumphant chuckle filling the room. And then he was beside her, his arm wrapping around her shoulder, his bloody hand pressing the knife blade against her throat. The smell of rotting, decaying things was breathing against her ear, filling her nostrils with an overpowering stench that she knew was not physical reality but, nonetheless, was real. It was his madness, she thought, and the odor was familiar. She let it overwhelm her because there was nothing she could do to prevent it, but one part of her mind, the part that could stand back from the horror and remember, identified it.

Her sister.

Frantically, as the thought clutched at her, she pushed it away. She could not afford to be pulled into the past now. *Not now.*

And then the almost-fragrant stench was a horrible whisper against her ear again, like the night the nightmare woke her with its scrabbling at the back of the neck.

"Bitch," came the hoarse whisper, "I've beat you. You ruined my life, and now you're going to pay for it, you know that?" There was a small, flesh-crawling chuckle. "You thought you had me, didn't you? And what about your whore? Did you like the way I had her?" The knife pressed insistently closer, and the whisper was more intense.

"Did you like her that way? Do you wish you had seen me do it to her?" And then the horrible chuckle again.

Stephanie tried to shrink from the blade. She swallowed and felt it touch her windpipe.

"What have I done to hurt you, Frank?" She had wanted her voice to be calming. It sounded terrified in her ears.

"Frank?" he said, and she saw his eyebrows lift sarcastically. "*Frank?* Like you *know* me, you cunt?" The hand holding her left shoulder squeezed cruelly, and she gasped from the pain.

Keep him talking, she thought. Keep him talking and give the police time. Give Marian time. She drew an agonizing breath between her lips, tried to fill her lungs.

"Are you sure you want to do this, Frank? You know, if you leave now, you can get out before the police get here. You could get away."

Talbot chuckled against her ear again. "Do you think that even matters now, bitch? I've got enough time anyway, but first, I'm going to kill your whore and let you watch."

Slowly he began to straighten, and she felt his grasp tighten on her upper arm so that he could pull her up. Her shoulder joint screamed with sudden pain. The knife was still at her throat. Time. She needed more time.

"Frank." She felt as if she were grabbing at straws. "Why did you kill Betty Jean?"

She heard a slight catch in his breath, as if the thought had interrupted his concentration. "Why did—?" She heard his thinking, as if he had forgotten the incident. Then comprehension seemed to dawn, the memory pulled from the tangled roots.

"She deserved to die," he said simply, as if he were making a comment about the weather. "You should know that."

He was pulling her to her feet, and she wanted to make her body limp, to make it harder for him, but her shoulder was crying out, and she had to cooperate a little just to take some of the strain off.

"Did the baby deserve to die, Frank?" she asked softly.

Talbot moved behind her, keeping the knife at her throat. "One less squalling brat."

"And how about your own?" His face was inches from her ear, and she felt his hot breath pummeling her skin.

"You're crazy, bitch. That whore wasn't going to have my kid. It was Danny's, or some other stupid jerk's."

Stephanie felt as if her lungs had run out of air again. She sucked in more through barely parted lips.

"But *she* is," Stephanie whispered, and she inclined her head slightly toward the living room door.

Talbot held onto the back of her neck with his free hand and kept the knife at her throat, but he moved so he was facing her. He stared at her. "Bullshit. You're just trying to rattle me."

Stephanie closed her eyes and made a nearly imperceptible shake of her head. She felt the blade against her skin, and she knew she was bleeding. She tried to sound bitter.

"She's going to leave me because I don't want the baby and she does, Frank."

Talbot stared at her, and she could almost hear his disbelief. There was a question, though, and it was like a door opening. Then the wall of disbelief rose again. She was losing. She felt helplessness rush through her in a wave.

"Good try, bitch. It won't work."

"It's true, Frank!" She stared into his eyes intently, as if willing him to know some awful truth. "That—" She made herself say it. "That *whore* is going to leave me, Frank. After all I've done, she's going to leave me because she wants to have your baby." She held her breath, waiting, hoping, but she knew suddenly that she was lost.

"Do you think I'm stupid?" he whispered harshly. "Do you think I'm *stupid*, bitch?" His eyes were like slits, and the hatred pumped out of them, swelled around her, pushed at her head, at her chest. In a moment, she would be unable to do anything. In one last desperate effort, she stepped to the side and clawed at the knife and the hand that held it.

But the shining steel was in front of her again, and the terror was crashing over her. "No," was all she could whisper through clenched teeth before she felt the knife plunge into her stomach. The pain brought a warm darkness swirling around her, taking her into its black chasm.

Marian huddled against the wall between the sofa and the end table that had been pushed back to give her room. She heard something heavy fall.

A body.

The thought crawled through her mind and brought horror

with it. Her arms and legs were tensed so tightly that it felt like every nerve ending was screaming at her.

Silence.

"Stef?" She whispered so softly that even she could barely hear it above the pounding of blood in her head.

And then the door on the other side of the living room, the door to Stephanie's office, was opening. When she saw with cold terror who stood in the doorway, his grin white in the dimness of the room, her body felt as if it had turned to ice.

With every once of her will, she made herself remain in the crouch that was making her legs ache with pain. She wanted to jump to her feet, run for the door to get away, run to Stephanie.

Stephanie.

The horror threatened to overtake her, and she put her knuckles to her mouth to stifle the scream. She made herself take a long, deep breath and tried to steady her hands.

Maybe Stephanie is dead. The possibility pounded in her chest.

Get control of yourself. Maybe she's just hurt. Maybe she's in another room and he didn't find her. Maybe the fall was Talbot stumbling against something. She couldn't afford to let that fear overtake her. Both her life and Stephanie's might depend on her now. She fought the panic that tried to surface.

Talbot took a slow step forward, and she saw him look around cautiously. Then she heard the horrible chuckle and whisper.

"Come on, baby, I know you're in here somewhere. The bitch is dead. Now we can do what we want to." He took another step. "Come on, baby. Come to papa," he whispered.

Marian's head rang with the sounds he was making, the obscene whisper that crawled up the back of her neck, made her head pound violently. She took a breath and tried to keep thoughts of Stephanie dead out of her mind as he came closer.

Stephanie is not dead, she screamed inside. *Stephanie is not dead. Stephanie is not...*

Talbot heard a soft noise from the corner of the sofa, and he grinned. There was a slight scraping sound, and he assumed she was moving back against the wall, further out of his sight as he came across the room. He took another step.

He put the knife down at his side so she wouldn't see it right away. She must know he had it, but maybe if she didn't see it, he could lure her out and it wouldn't be such a hard struggle.

He was running out of time.

Then, suddenly, as he stepped past the coffee table, he saw her, huddled beside the sofa, squeezed in between the sofa and end table. She was sitting on her haunches, staring at him, her eyes huge in the darkness of the room, the terror clear on her face, her hands sort of folded and squeezed between her thighs.

He held out his left hand as if to invite her to come with him, and he felt a wide smile touch his mouth. The cat had found the last of the mice.

"Come on, baby," he whispered. "I won't hurt you again." His voice was honeyed and soft. "You'll see. I'll be good to you."

He waited a moment, then he heard her voice. It startled him. It was low, seductive, soft like his own.

"You want me, Frank?"

His eyes narrowed. It was too easy. His hands started sweating again. He wiped his left palm on his pants. But maybe he had been wrong. Maybe the bitch had told him the truth. Maybe the whore really didn't want some lezzie bitch pawing at her any more.

He had to see her face. Her eyes. If he could just see her eyes, he'd know the truth. He reached into his pocket and pulled out his lighter. He thumbed the wheel on the lighter, and in the flickering light, he saw her face then. The terror was beautiful to him, the fear that played across her eyes, her full mouth. He felt power surging through his body.

But as he reached out his hand toward the woman huddled in front of him, he felt that cold finger making its way up the back of his neck again, that terrible, scrabbling, crawling sensation. He turned slowly, horrified as he heard the knob turn on the door across the living room.

In the doorway, the bitch stood looking at him, holding her stomach, her face in the shadows so he could not see her. He felt the hair prickle on his scalp.

"*You're dead,*" he rasped. His mouth was dry, his throat almost closed.

And then, there was another sound from the woman perched

beside the sofa. He jerked back, and in the light from the flickering lighter, he saw that her hands had risen from between her thighs and that she had a gun pointed at his face. He put out a hand to stop her as the hammer was pulled back to cock the gun, but the fear clawing at the back of his neck stopped him from moving to avoid the explosion. He waited there, waited for the sound that would rip through his skull when the gun was fired.

But there was no explosion. There was only the fear that clawed insistently at the back of his neck, and he whimpered with the terror it brought.

It was the old nightmare again. There were eyes all around him, floating toward him, coming at him, and then drifting to his side where he couldn't see them. They swam toward him, crowded in on him, smothered him with their closeness. He flailed at them with his arms, stabbed at them with his knife, but they were always just out of his reach, mocking him. He couldn't breathe.

He backed toward the door, trying to escape them. But they were sticking to him now, like leeches, on his clothes, his skin. He heard soft, childlike, whimpering sounds, and when he realized who was making them, he tried to stop himself. He brushed at the eyes that were stuck on his pants, his shirt. He picked at the ones on the back of his hand. But he couldn't get them off.

Finally he felt the door against his back, and he clawed at the key, his hands so slippery with sweat that the key seemed to whirl crazily in the lock. He screamed as he felt an eye brush against his cheek, slimy, warm in the darkness.

Then, suddenly, he heard the bolt click back. He yanked the door open, and fresh, cool air struck his face. He staggered onto the porch and pulled in huge gulps.

It was then that he noticed the lights. They were bright. Too bright for the streetlight. Monsters' eyes, he thought wildly. Monsters' eyes pointed at him from every direction. A monster was charging at him from his left, and he whirled and stabbed madly at the air.

The explosion from the young officer's gun picked him up as if he were a child's doll and flung him back across the porch. As his body slammed into the wall and sagged to the concrete slab, the tormenting eyes winked into a final blackness.

Epilog

1988
Sunday
9
October

Fireflies winked on and off in the slight breeze that stirred across Matanzas Bay and drifted up from the inlet. Stephanie sighed in contentment and sank more deeply into the lawn chair.

"That picnic table looks like a swarm of locusts visited our backyard and brought all their cousins," Marian said as she slumped lazily in the chair next to Stephanie's.

"And there's still so much food left, we'll be eating it for a week," Stephanie murmured. She sighed. "Any minute now, I'm going to get up and start cleaning."

Marian groaned. "God, no. I can't move." She turned her head toward Stephanie. "And you don't look like you'll be up and around for a while either, my dear."

"I acquiesce. Gladly."

Out by the vegetable garden, Gary stood beside the late-summer tomatoes and pointed out something to the light-haired young woman who stood beside him. Jenny smiled and hooked her arm through his.

Stephanie glanced at Marian and saw the smile that played across her mouth as she watched Gary and Jenny. She was looking fine these days, Stephanie mused, full of plans for her classes and what she would be planting in their winter garden. The small dark circles under her eyes had disappeared, and her laughter had been coming more easily in the past weeks.

Stephanie smiled in response and closed her eyes. Gary and Jenny laughed somewhere far away, and she heard Marian humming some tune, distant somehow. She allowed her mind to drift. It was summer again. Maybe two years from now.

Jenny and Gary were at the edge of the backyard, but now they were playing with a little boy. They laughed as he wriggled out of Gary's grasp and ran toward Stephanie and Marian. As he reached them, he patted them both on the leg and squealed delightedly, his chubby toddler's legs still a little wobbly.

Marian laughed with him. His curly black hair glinted in the sunlight, and blue-green eyes as deep as Marian's own twinkled up at her. Leaning over, Stephanie caught him up and balanced him on her knee. He patted her face and squealed with delight again. She stared into his eyes, searching, and then smiled. There was nothing behind his laughter but pure love. She held him while Marian played their this-little-piggy game with his bare toes and he giggled at her.

Suddenly, she felt Marian's hand on her shoulder, and she started. She opened her eyes and patted Marian's hand. Marian would begin showing soon, she thought.

"Where were you, hon?"

Stephanie smiled. "Tomorrow," she murmured. "I was thinking about tomorrow."

"Well, if all the smiling you were doing is any indication, I'd say it's going to be a great place to be."

"Mmm." She squeezed Marian's hand. "I think I have an ending for your story now."

Marian's voice took on a playfully seductive tone. "I don't have classes tomorrow, and I've got time for a very long bedtime story. Promise you'll tell me tonight?"

Stephanie grinned. "You would let me refuse? You wouldn't try to persuade me?"

Marian's eyes twinkled, and she entwined their fingers. "My love," she laughed softly, "you know me better than that."

Other books of interest from
ALYSON PUBLICATIONS

Don't miss our FREE BOOK offer at the end of this section.

☐ **WANDERGROUND,** by Sally Miller Gearhart, $7.00. Here are stories of the hill women, who combine the control of mind and matter with a sensuous adherence to women's realities and history. A lesbian classic.

☐ **A FEMINIST TAROT,** by Sally Miller Gearhart and Susan Rennie, $7.00. The first tarot book to emerge from the women's movement, with interpretations of tarot cards that reflect women's experiences in contemporary society.

☐ **CHOICES,** by Nancy Toder, $8.00. This popular novel about lesbian love depicts the joy, passion, conflicts and intensity of love between women as Nancy Toder conveys the fear and confusion of a woman coming to terms with her sexual and emotional attraction to other women.

☐ **THE PEARL BASTARD,** by Lillian Halegua, $4.00. Frankie is fifteen when she leaves her large, suffocating Catholic family. Here, with painful innocence and acute vision, she tells the story of her sudden entry into a harsh maturity, beginning with the man in the fine green car who does not mourn the violent death of a seagull against his windshield.

☐ **THE TWO OF US,** by Larry Uhrig, $7.00. The author draws on his years of counseling with gay people to give some down-to-earth advice about what makes a relationship work. He gives special emphasis to the religious aspects of gay unions.

☐ **LIFETIME GUARANTEE,** by Alice Bloch, $7.00. Here is the personal and powerfully-written chronicle of a woman faced with the impending death of her sister from cancer, at the same time that she must also face her family's reaction to her as a lesbian.

☐ **DANCER DAWKINS AND THE CALIFORNIA KID,** by Willyce Kim, $6.00. Dancer Dawkins would like to just sit back and view life from behind a pile of hotcakes. But her lover, Jessica Riggins, has fallen into the clutches of Fatin Satin Aspen, and something must be done. Meanwhile, Little Willie Gutherie of Bangor, Maine, renames herself The California Kid, stocks up on Rubbles Dubble bubble gum, and heads west. When this crew collides in San Francisco, what can be expected? Just about anything. . . .

☐ **THE LAW OF RETURN,** by Alice Bloch, $8.00. The widely-praised novel of a woman who, returning to Israel, regains her Jewish heritage while also claiming her voice as a woman and as a lesbian. "Clear, warm, haunting and inspired" writes Phyllis Chesler. "I want to read everything Alice Bloch writes," adds Grace Paley.

☐ **BETWEEN FRIENDS,** by Gillian E. Hanscombe, $7.00. Frances and Meg were friends in school years ago; now Frances is a married housewife while Meg is a lesbian involved in progressive politics. Through letters written between these women and their friends, the author weaves an engrossing story while exploring many vital lesbian and feminist issues.

☐ **COMING TO POWER: Writings and graphics on lesbian S/M,** edited by Samois, $9.00. Few issues have divided the lesbian-feminist community as much as that of S/M practices among lesbians; here are essays, stories, pictures and personal testimony from members of Samois, the San Francisco lesbian-feminist S/M group.

☐ **LONG TIME PASSING: Lives of Older Lesbians,** edited by Marcy Adelman, $8.00. Here, in their own words, women talk about age related concerns: the fear of losing a lover; the experiences of being a lesbian in the 1940s and 1950s; and issues of loneliness and community.

☐ **DEAR SAMMY: Letters from Gertrude Stein and Alice B. Toklas,** by Samuel M. Steward, $8.00. As a young man, Samuel M. Steward journeyed to France to meet the two women he so admired. It was the beginning of a long friendship. Here he combines his fascinating memoirs of Toklas and Stein with photos and more than a hundred of their letters.

☐ **TALK BACK! A gay person's guide to media action, $4.00.** When were you last outraged by prejudiced media coverage of gay people? Chances are it hasn't been long. This short, highly readable book tells how you, in surprisingly little time, can do something about it.

To get these books:

Ask at your favorite bookstore for the books listed here. You may also order by mail. Just fill out the coupon below, or use your own paper if you prefer not to cut up this book.

GET A FREE BOOK! When you order any three books listed here at the regular price, you may request a *free* copy of *Légende*.

— — — — — — — — — — — — — — — —

Enclosed is $_____ for the following books. (Add $1.00 postage when ordering just one book; if you order two or more, we'll pay the postage.)

1. _____

2. _____

3. _____

4. _____

5. _____

☐ Send a free copy of *Légende* as offered above. I have ordered at least three other books.

name:_____

address: _____

city:_____state:_____zip:_____

ALYSON PUBLICATIONS
Dept. H-23, 40 Plympton St., Boston, Mass. 02118

This offer expires Dec. 31, 1990. After that date, please write for current catalog.